BUCKWHE
SUMMER

What can a farm family do when they are hailed out in the middle of summer? "It is too late to sow wheat or corn," the menfolk agreed. Mr. Martin decided to try buckwheat, but nobody in the family had ever seen buckwheat except in the shape of buckwheat pancakes.

To Martha Martin, this was one of the minor problems of the summer. A more important one was that she needed a friend. There was a Polish girl just her age down the road, but there were many good reasons why Martha could not make friends with Stefana Baronski.

In the first place, Stefana's brothers had stolen a calf from the Martin farm. Or if they had not, what had happened to Rosebud?

There was another reason why Martha would not make friends with Stefana, but this reason Martha would not admit, even to herself.

Martha had another problem: How could she make her family realize that she was a Somebody, not just a sister to be ordered around and teased, but Somebody Important? Every time Martha tried to prove to her family how talented she was, something happened to spoil the effect.

Her brother Arnold was a terrible problem. He called her greenish-brown eyes "cat eyes." Her older brother Paul was a problem, too. He had been going with Mary Miller for six years. When was he going to announce their engagement? Her sister Janie was obviously too young to be of help with these important problems.

So everyone had solutions for her and the buckwheat summer was full of surprises, but Martha was most surprised by the things she learned about herself.

BUCKWHEAT SUMMER

BUCKWHEAT SUMMER By Ruth Unrau

HERALD PRESS,

SCOTTDALE, PENNSYLVANIA

For

Susan and Paula

Martha and Carol

When they say, "Tell us about the time

When you were a little girl."

203

THE CALENDAR

CHAPTER 1

Monday, July 10
THE DREARY DAY

MARTHA MARTIN lay in her bed, more awake than asleep, dreaming that she was a nurse. Noiselessly she moved from bed to bed in the hospital ward; she was beautiful and efficient in her white uniform as she touched her cool hand to fevered brows.

The brows belonged to the five other members of the Martin family, all in the hospital with broken legs. She was their sole source of comfort.

"Can this be our Martha?" they asked one another.

The dream changed, and Martha was playing a great piano masterpiece that she had composed. She finished playing with a crashing chord. The audience cheered and applauded. Bouquets of roses were thrown at her feet.

In this remarkable dream, her family sat in the front row, clapping wildly. Her brother Arnold shouted, "Hurrah for Martha. She has made our family famous."

The dream changed again, and as her admiring family watched, Martha climbed into the cockpit of an airplane for a flight around the world. She soared into the sky, up, up, and up. At this point, Martha Martin, girl aviator, fell out of bed.

Then Martha awakened fully and became aware of life

9

as it really was. Instead of the bright lights of the concert hall, there was the sun shining through the east window, too warm on her face. Instead of a family showering her with applause, there was only Janie.

And Janie, as usual, had taken more than her share of the bed. She curled, unbudging and unawakable, in the very middle.

At this point Martha remembered that her most important trouble had nothing to do with the sun or with Janie. The dreary fact was that half a summer stretched ahead of her with no place to go, nothing to do, and nobody to come visiting. Sundays were good days, but today was Monday. The week ahead looked long and dull.

Martha knew what her mother would say about her attitude: "Martha, you are just spoiled. You've had this nice long vacation at Grandma's since school was out, and now that you're home, you don't know what to do with yourself."

Martha admitted that that was part of the problem. Now that her vacation was over, there was nothing to look forward to. Well, yes, there was. In a month the Martin family was to take a trip to Colorado to visit Aunt Louise, and Martha could hardly wait. How would she ever live through the next four weeks?

Martha lay for a moment letting the dreariness of life wash over her. Life was not only dreary; it was dead, dull, dry, dopey, and disappointing.

"If only I had a friend who lived close by, we could have fun. I don't see why our farm has to be away from everybody."

By *everybody,* Martha meant the girls in sixth grade at Indian Grove School. For the moment, she refused to remember that Stefana Baronski lived just a half mile down the road. Stefana was her mortal—or immortal—enemy.

There was no sound downstairs. Martha slipped out of bed and dressed quickly. Down at the kitchen sink she splashed her face with pump water and gave her dark bangs a flick with the comb. She took a brief glance in the small mirror over the sink. As usual, her reflection surprised her. Martha always thought of herself as a dark-haired, brown-eyed, indescribably lovely girl. The mirror reminded her that she looked rather ordinary. Her mouth was too wide and her nose too tilted for beauty. And her eyes! Her eyes were an awful greenish-brown.

"If only Arnold wouldn't call them cat eyes, I could bear them."

A strange voice outside the door caught her ear. Martha stepped quickly to the screen door. Her mother was standing by the garden gate talking to a man who had his back to Martha. She recognized him by his mixture of Polish and English and by his broad shoulders. He was the older of the Baronski brothers, and he was gesturing wildly to Mrs. Martin. He might have been scooping with an invisible shovel, then throwing whatever he had scooped high into the sky.

When the flow of strange sounds and motions stopped, Mamma nodded her head and said, slowly and distinctly, "Let's look in the calf shed. I think we'll find one there."

The two walked off toward the barn.

"Now what business does he have here?" Martha asked herself. "I wish those terrible Baronskis would stay home."

She turned back to the kitchen. There was still the smell of pancakes, but the food had been put away. The unwashed breakfast dishes were stacked on the table. Martha set out her own breakfast of sugared cherries, milk, bread, and butter.

While she ate, she read an article in *Hoard's Dairyman* on the feeding of calves. "I wonder if Arnie has tried feeding Rosebud this Kaffmeal." Arnold was very particular about Rosebud's diet, for he said that the food made a difference between a winner and a loser. Martha doubted if he could afford Kaffmeal.

"Marty, are you up?" Janie called from upstairs.

"For hours. Come, get some breakfast."

Janie appeared in her nightgown, brown hair tousled, brown eyes still sleepy. "Why didn't you call me? Everybody is up but 'cept me."

Martha said automatically, "Except, not but 'cept. Want some cherries?"

Martha helped Janie start her breakfast; then she went to sit on the back steps. This was always a shady spot. A large box elder tree grew near the back porch and the porch swing had been hung from its lowest branch.

Martha's mother came from the barnyard and called, "Good morning, Martha. Have you had your breakfast?"

"Yes, Mamma. Janie is eating hers now. What did the Baronski boy want?"

"They are making hay and they need another pitchfork. He wanted to borrow ours. I had a time understanding him, but I finally caught on to his sign language." Mrs. Martin picked up her hoe and went into the kitchen garden.

Martha went to sit in the garden path to watch her mother hoe weeds. Green beans were just coming on and the early tomatoes were ripening. The flowers were at their best, brilliant and bountiful. Beyond the garden, the orchard was heavy with fruit. The Transparent apples, pale yellow, were just right for sauce. The cherries were at their best, big and bright red.

"It's like a picture, isn't it?" Martha said.

"What is like a picture?" Mamma had not been reading Martha's mind.

"The garden. It is just like a picture in the seed catalog."

Mamma straightened from her hoeing to look around. "Yes, this has been a wonderful year to farm. The crops are all good." She pushed a large bone hairpin more firmly into her bun of black hair and went back to her hoeing.

A cloud drifted over them, and Martha looked up. "Hey, I thought the sun was shining."

"The radio said scattered showers for today; so I didn't wash this morning. We really don't need the rain, though. I think we have had more this summer than in any summer since we moved to Indiana." Elmer and Mattie Martin had moved to Indiana about twenty years ago. They had come from Iowa to settle in the newly drained Kankakee Valley.

Martha sat for a few minutes watching the bright poppy petals shatter in the breeze.

"Mamma, what shall I do?"

"Dishes, maybe?" her mother suggested.

"I don't mean dishes. Or I mean *after* I do dishes. I don't have anybody to play with and there's nothing fun to do. I wish I had a sister or brother. Life is so dreary."

"Grandma spoiled you. Now it is hard for you to settle down to ordinary life."

"I knew you would say that."

"Why don't you see if Stefana can play with you? That isn't too far to ride the pony. Or you could even walk," Mamma suggested.

True, Stefana Baronski lived close enough to visit easily. But Martha wasn't about to go visit her, neither did she want to meet up with the wild-looking Baronski brothers.

"I just don't feel like playing with Stefana," Martha said.

"I'm surprised that you haven't ever been to visit Stefana. I though when the Baronskis moved in last March that you would probably spend half your time down there."

"I don't know her very well," was all Martha would say, and that was true enough. Her mother looked at her thoughtfully.

Martha persisted, "Don't you have any other ideas for something to do besides dishes—or piano practicing?"

Her mother laughed. "Well, if you have time after you get the dishes washed, you can set the table for dinner."

Martha could not see that there was anything humorous about dishes. Of course, sometimes she was slow getting started, but to say that dishwashing took all morning was aggravating! She went inside to hurry Janie with her breakfast.

To Janie she said crossly, "Hurry up, slowpoke, so you can dry."

Janie deliberately spooned the last of her bread and milk soup into her mouth before answering. "Anyway, I'm a fast slowpoke."

As Martha did not have a reply for such hopeless logic,

she started on the dishes. "I wonder if Stefana has to do a million dishes a day," she said to Janie as she sloshed the suds around in the pan.

Janie protested, "You don't have a million dishes to do. I doubt if you have more than ten thousand." Janie liked to be exact, but her grasp of large numbers was hazy.

"A million, billion, trillion, what's the difference?" Martha replied. "Of course, there are only five in her family and there are six in ours."

To herself she thought, "Why worry about Stefana Baronski, anyway? I don't care *how* many dishes she has to do." Martha scrubbed the sticky pancake syrup off the plates.

It was ten o'clock by the time Martha finished cleaning up the kitchen. By then the rain had started. Mamma came hurrying in from the garden. She stopped on the back porch to take off her garden shoes and to wipe the rain off her face with her apron.

"Papa and the boys are going to be soaked by the time they come in from the cornfield," she predicted.

Ten minutes later the three Martin men trooped onto the back porch and called for dry clothes.

"I feel like a wet muskrat," Paul said. He had had lots of experience trapping wet muskrats.

"Skin yourselves right there," Mamma said. "I'll bring you some dry clothes. Just don't drip all over the house."

"What did Thaddeus Baronski want?" Arnold asked, wiping the rain from his glasses. "I saw him drive in here."

Martha answered him while Mamma was getting the clothes. "He needed a pitchfork. She gave him the one in the calf shed."

"Did he see Rosebud? What did he think of her?" Arnold asked.

Mamma started passing out overalls and shirts to her menfolk. "Yes, he saw her. He thought she was a fine-looking calf."

"Let's have an early dinner," Papa suggested. "Maybe we can get back to the field if it doesn't rain too hard."

14

Mamma said with a laugh, *"Früher Sturm und tanzende Grossmütterchen halten nicht lange vor."*

"Tell us what you said," Martha begged.

Mamma quoted: "Early storm and dancing grandmother don't last very long."

However, the old German proverb did not prove true. The rain did not stop until noon, and by then the fields were too wet to work in. Since they could not plow, the men busied themselves around the barns after dinner.

Paul, who had received an old car for his recent twenty-first birthday, went to the garage to do some tinkering. His blue coupé had taken him and Mary Miller to Chicago last Saturday. They had gone to the World's Fair and had brought Martha a spoon inscribed "Chicago World's Fair, 1933." Although the car had made the eighty-mile trip without any trouble, Paul wanted to check her over.

Arnold, as always when he had free time, went to groom his 4-H calf. The calf had got stuck with the name of Rosebud, and Arnold thought that this was a sissy name. But, as Mamma asked, "What better name is there for a calf whose mother's name is Rose? Rosette? Rosella?" Arnold would have preferred Queen Elizabeth, or Champion of Martin Acres, or something very dignified.

After they finished the dishes, Martha and Janie went to find Arnold. He was sitting on the railing in the calf shed. His hands were busy tying knots in a rope while he watched Rosebud.

"Isn't she the most beautiful calf you ever laid eyes on?" Arnold asked the girls. "No other calf at the fair will be able to touch her."

"For a calf I guess she'll do. I don't know as I would call her beautiful." Martha hadn't come to discuss calves. "Come and carry some cement blocks for us. We want to build a playhouse behind the corncrib."

Janie added her plea. "Come on, Arnie. Please?"

But Arnold couldn't be bothered. "I'm busy. I have to brush her down." He slid off the railing and took up the currycomb. "Anyway, you have enough playhouses around this place. Go clean up your old ones."

Martha resented Arnold's bossy tone. "You're so smart," she flung at him. "Come, Janie."

Even if Arnold was sixteen, he wasn't grown-up, she told herself. In fact, he was small and slight for his age. Martha did not see why he should always treat her as though he were a man and she a child. He made her so mad!

The girls wandered outside again. Their father passed by as they came out the door of the calf shed.

"Be sure to hook that door from the outside," he called. "That Rosebud has got so smart she can lift the inside hook with her nose."

Martha left the top part of the door open, but she hooked the bottom door on both the inside and the outside. Then the girls went to see what they could do about a playhouse. Janie looked at the mud puddles in the barnyard and suggested that they looked like rooms; so they used the whole place for a playhouse, splashing from room to room in their very wet house.

At supper that evening Arnold asked, "Do you think we can plow again tomorrow, Pa?"

Papa took a large helping of tomatoes and sugared them generously. "Well, I doubt if it will be dry enough before noon, much as I would like to get that corn plowed."

"I would like to take my calf over to the elevator to weigh her. I need to enter her weight in my record book."

Mamma said, "Since Arnold got his driver's license, he can think of so many reasons for driving around."

"I can drive," Janie said. "Paul let me sit on his lap and drive yesterday. When can I get a license?"

"How old are you now?" asked Paul.

"I was five in May."

"Well, when you are sixteen, you can get a license."

"Next year, then, I guess," Janie said, her brown eyes full of mischief.

Everyone laughed at Janie's joke.

Martha thought, "Everyone thinks Janie is cute, but they never pay any attention to me. Why is five a cute age and eleven not?" Aloud she said, "When I was five, did I look like Janie?"

Paul answered, "No, but you were a cute little tyke." Then as though he had read her mind, "Eleven is a nice age, I think."

Martha had never thought of eleven as a nice age; she longed to be twelve and grown-up. However, it was nice of Paul to say that. He was a grownup. He treated Martha with respect as though she, too, were grown-up, or almost.

"Let's finish the chores," Papa said, rising from the table.

At that moment there was a knock at the front door. Everyone looked surprised, because only strangers came to the front door. Everyone else came right to the back door where they could expect to find the family.

Papa went to the door, which opened into the living room, and the rest of the family followed.

"Hello, Mr. Martin," Martha heard a strange voice say. "I am looking for the Baronski farm. Can you tell me where to find it?"

"Why, yes, next house down the road west of here. Kind of up on a hill."

"Thank you. Quite a rain we had, wasn't it?"

"It was a real soaker. Hope we don't have any more for a while now."

Martha became very impatient while they went on to talk about crops and weather. When finally the man left and Papa came back in, Martha looked out of the window to watch the stranger get into his car.

His black car was parked out on the road, but Martha could easily read the large white letters printed on the door:

Sheriff
Pleasant County

"Pa, what does the sheriff want with the Baronskis?" asked Arnold, who was looking over Martha's shoulder.

17

"Didn't say, and I didn't ask," and Mr. Martin refused to offer any theories.

"I suppose somebody up there broke a law," Arnold decided, as he followed his father and Paul out to do their chores.

Martha went to help her mother with the dishes. It didn't surprise her that the sheriff was looking for the Baronskis. They were just the type who would get into trouble with the law.

CHAPTER 2

Tuesday, July 11
SUMMER STORM

MARTHA decided that she would play through "Moonlight and Starlight" just once more. Then she would quit practicing for the day. She played the piece rapidly, ending with a great explosion of chords.

Her mother popped her head through the doorway to ask, "My! did the star come crashing down to earth?"

"No, the moon just exploded," Martha explained.

She wandered outside to find something to do to fill the long hours until suppertime. Summer was a horrible time with nothing to do.

"I wish I had a sister my age," she told herself for the seventy-fifth time that summer. She sat down in the swing so that she could feel sorry for herself in comfort.

"Yes, I really need another sister, but a brother my age would do, if he would play with me," she thought. "On the other hand, brothers are awful teases," she reminded herself.

Take Arnold, for example. He was a terrible tease. But worse than his teasing was his bossiness. True, he was five years older than she was, but she refused to take orders from him.

"Go upstairs and get my blue necktie," he would say sometimes.

Martha would answer, very cleverly, she thought, "Who was your step-and-fetch-it last year?"

Then Arnold would get mad. "You're afraid to do anything for anybody, aren't you? Just wait until you want me to do something for you. Just wait."

This bickering would go on and on, each of them trying to be the most insulting. Finally Papa would say, "That's enough of that. Remember that you are Christians, and Christians don't fight."

"Oh, Papa," Martha would protest. "You mean that we shouldn't go to war. Arnold and I aren't planning to go to war."

Her father shook his head. "No, I mean that we are to get along with everybody, even our brothers and sisters."

But Martha had long ago decided that she couldn't possibly get along with Arnold. Paul was different. He was her best friend in the family. But since he was ten years older than she, he was not a playmate.

Martha had never before explored the idea of having a brother near her own age, and so she sat on the swing on this July day and dreamed of how much fun she would have with a brother twelve years old. She would jump from a high place in the haymow and her make-believe brother (what should she call him? Gilbert, after Anne's hero in *Anne of Green Gables*), Gilbert, would say admiringly, "My, what a brave girl you are!"

Well, she didn't have an admiring brother, but there was Delcie Birky. Delcie wasn't a brother. She wasn't even a boy, but she was admiring and she was a tomboy. Wasn't it too bad that her cousin lived eight miles away and they could get together only on Sundays? If only the Birkys lived where the Baronskis lived.

Martha thought of her mother's often-asked question: "Why don't you play with Stefana?" but she put it out of her mind. Or she *tried* to put the question out of her mind. Her conscience was likely to be quite prickly when Stefana's name was mentioned.

The Baronskis had moved onto the Craig place in March. The Craig farm changed tenants often. Although the land was fairly good, the house and other buildings were very poor; therefore, tenants moved as soon as they could find a good farm with better buildings. It was Martha's yearly wish that someone would move onto the Craig farm who would become a best friend. The Craig farm was a convenient distance from the Martin farm. Two friends living that close together would be able to see each other every day and share every experience.

Martha often imagined the conversations she might have with such a friend.

Annabelle (this was Martha's favorite name) would say, "Martha, I just love your hair. I have always wanted dark hair." Annabelle would carefully avoid any mention of greenish-brown eyes.

And Martha would say, "Oh, I hate and despise my hair. But you have such lovely blond curls."

Annabelle would love to read. They would discuss with each other all the books they read.

Annabelle had never come to live on the Craig farm. Stefana Baronski had come, but Martha knew that she could never be a best friend.

Mr. Baronski and the two boys had worked in the steel mills in Gary for five years. They had decided to try farming, for they had been farmers in Poland before coming to America. Mr. Baronski had told Papa that they had been happy to get back on the farm. Although they did not have much equipment, they were slowly building up their supply of machinery and livestock.

Talking with the Baronskis was difficult. Only Stefana could speak good English. The rest of the family mixed Polish and English and used Polish when they became excited. In Gary they had lived with friends from their own country and had not learned American ways.

Stefana was the only one of the three children still in school. She had caused quite a sensation when she had appeared at Indian Grove that first morning, wearing a black dress and long black stockings. Martha had felt sorry for the outlandish child with the blond braids.

Dorothy Johnson had said that first day, "Doesn't she look stupid, though?"

In a way, Stefana acted a little strange, too. At recess she stayed in the schoolroom unless Miss Williams made her play outside. Stefana could not jump rope or roller skate or play ball. When it came to running games like blackman or dare-base, she was good enough. She could run fast. But when the girls played house under the big oak tree, Stefana sat back and watched.

"She just isn't a bit friendly," Dorothy Johnson complained. "Why doesn't she come play with us?"

"Maybe she is just shy," Martha said.

One day as they were gathering acorn shells for the playhouse, Dorothy confided to Martha: "I hear that they speak Polish at home," making it sound as though a person who spoke Polish would also eat peas with her knife.

"Wouldn't you think they would have learned English by this time?" Martha answered.

They heard a movement behind them, and they turned in time to see Stefana slip around the corner of the woodshed. Undoubtedly she had overheard them discussing her family. Martha was sorry that Stefana might have had her feelings hurt.

"I still say she's dumb," Dorothy insisted.

Martha had felt that the girls were sometimes rude to Stefana during those last months of school. This unkindness was not right, she knew. She herself had never been rude. She just had not gone out of her way to be friendly.

Stefana had been at Indian Grove for a month when Martha suddenly woke up to an important fact. Stefana might look stupid, but there was nothing stupid about her mind. For Martha, this was a painful discovery.

Martha had always been at the top of her class, and it had always been easy for her to stay ahead of her classmates.

Then in April she realized that Stefana had not missed a word in spelling since she had come. Martha had not missed any either, but the idea that there was someone in the class who was as good as Martha was a shock. In geography if Stefana missed a question, so did everyone else.

It was in arithmetic, however, where Stefana proved her ability. Arithmetic was Martha's weakest subject. She always mastered it, but often her mother had to help her with it.

Miss Williams had once told Martha as she handed back a poor paper, "Martha, I think you could be a writer, or a schoolteacher, or President of the United States, but I don't think you should aim for a career in engineering."

Martha had not planned for a career in engineering. She wasn't really sure what an engineer did, but she guessed it must have something to do with arithmetic.

On the other hand, Stefana was as good in arithmetic as she was in spelling. Martha wondered if Miss Williams had advised her to be an engineer.

It was at this time that Martha stopped feeling sorry for Stefana. A girl who could make such good grades in arithmetic did not need pity. It is not easy to be friendly with someone who is a better student than you are.

Therefore, as the school year drew to a close, Martha found that her position at the head of the class was in danger.

Each year Miss Williams gave a certificate of merit to the best student in each class. In the fifth grade, of course, everyone looked to Martha Martin as the best student. She had four certificates from past years in her top dresser drawer that proved that she was best. Other boys and girls could bat and catch better than she could, and most could draw and sing better. Martha's one claim to fame at Indian Grove was her ability to make good grades. She planned to get six certificates, one for each year at Indian Grove. That would be a record that even Arnold could not match, as he had received only four. Mamma blamed the teacher for not getting him started right in reading, but just the same, he had not won six certificates.

Martha wished she had kept closer count of Stefana's grades and compared them with her own. Stefana had a high average, she knew.

"Sure Stefana is smart," Dorothy Johnson finally admitted. "But she isn't as smart as you are. Anyway, she has been here only ten weeks. I'll bet she didn't get such good grades in Gary as she does here."

On the last day of school when report cards were handed out and the certificates were presented, Martha waited impatiently to hear her name called. Miss Williams stood at her desk at the front of the room and called each student up to receive his certificate.

"First grade—John Howard Good." Johnny Good was almost too shy to go up in front of all the students. Everyone clapped loudly for Johnny.

"Second grade—Carrie Lou Johnson." Again everyone clapped as Dorothy's little sister ran up to claim her certificate.

"Third grade—Thelma Fowler. . . . Fourth grade—Ernestine Hofer." And Ernestine, whom the boys called Hofer the Heifer, proudly claimed her award.

Martha slid forward to the edge of her seat so that she could rise gracefully to walk up the aisle.

"Fifth grade—" Miss Williams' voice took on a note of warmth and she smiled with pleasure. "Fifth grade—Stefana Baronski."

There was a hush as Stefana started toward Miss Williams' desk. Martha quickly slid back into her seat, hoping that no one had seen that she had almost made a fool of herself. Someone started to applaud then, and everyone clapped twice as loud for Stefana to make up for their slow start. Stefana came back to her desk, her cheeks pink with excitement. As she passed Martha's desk, she gave her a quick look of triumph.

Martha understood the look completely. It said, "So, Martha Martin, my folks speak Polish at home, but I can make good grades, too."

Martha decided right then that, no matter what, she would never like Stefana Baronski or try to make friends with her.

"We are immortal enemies," Martha had vowed as she walked home from school that last day, "or is it mortal enemies? Anyway, we are enemies till death do us part."

That was why Martha swung aimlessly in the swing on a summer day with no one to play with.

No brother, no sister, no friend. Martha felt as though she were completely alone in the world. If only Stefana—

"I wonder what Stefana would be like if I got to know her well," Martha asked herself.

Would it be worth going down there to try to find out? Then the memory of Stefana's face as she held the certificate of merit came back to her mind, and Martha gave up the idea. Anyway, she was scared of those brothers.

It was only three o'clock and hours until suppertime. Martha decided that there was nothing to do but start on *Penrod* for the third time. Since this was an emergency, she got two of the caramels she had stored away and settled down with her book.

The men came in for an early supper again that evening because they had not been able to work in the wet fields. After the chores were taken care of and the kitchen cleaned up, everyone gathered in the dining room.

Paul wrote a letter, Martha supposed to Mary Miller, although he had seen her only last Sunday. Arnold and Janie wrestled on the rug. Martha lay on the floor reading the last chapter of *Penrod*.

"Arnold, would you like to make some fudge?" Mamma asked. "You haven't made any for a long time."

Arnold liked to cook, and fudge was his specialty. He and Janie agreed that fudge would be good, but they did not feel ambitious enough to get off the floor and make it.

"Let go my head or I'll throw you to the top of the windmill and let you wave around like a flag," Arnold threatened.

"Leggo my leg, or I'll throw *you* in the horse tank," Janie countered good-naturedly. "Then Pet and Bess will drink you right up."

Arnold dumped her in a heap on the window seat. He picked up his rope book from the table and pulled a length of rope from his pocket. When he had settled himself cross-legged on the floor with the book of instructions in front of him, he began tying knots. This had been his latest interest and he practiced often.

"This is a funny evening," Martha said. "Usually the men work until the sun goes down. Here we are finished with supper and it is still light."

But even as she was speaking, the sun went behind a dark cloud. Presently the rain spattered timidly outside the open door.

Papa looked up from his newspaper. "More rain? We don't need it."

Paul said, "My forty is going to have weeds taller than the corn." Paul had rented a neighboring field to farm for himself. He was trying to save money so that he could start farming on his own. Although no one in the family had said so directly, Martha had the idea that Paul wanted very much to get married—to Mary Miller, of course.

Martha listened as the rain grew louder. Lightning flashed through the dining room, followed immediately by an explosion of thunder.

Papa asked, "You fastened the barn door, didn't you, Arnold? You don't want your calf to get out."

"Sure, I fastened it. I always do."

The rain turned to hail. First there was a rattle against the screens, then a pounding as the hail beat on the west side of the house. Arnold ran upstairs to shut the west windows.

"That sounds terrible," Mamma said. "It will knock all the apples off the trees."

"It's a good thing we have screens on our windows," Arnold said, coming back to the dining room. "That hail sounds as though it could crash right through the glass."

Soon the noise of the hail let up. Then there were only occasional thumps as it tapered off.

"At any rate, it didn't last long," Paul said. "Let's go see how it looks outside."

They all went out into the back yard to look things over. In the twilight they could see that the hail had done some damage.

"Look at my poor garden," Mamma wailed as she picked up a bruised tiger lily. The blossoms had been knocked off many of the flowers and some of the tomato vines were broken. Everything looked ragged and bent.

Janie was delighted with the ice. "Summer ice! How nice! Icy nice," she chanted as she picked up a panful to take into the house.

They all went back to the dining room again to discuss the hail damage.

Papa said, "Don't think it hurt the corn too much."

Mamma was cheerful. "I'm counting on that corn to take us to Colorado. Don't let anything happen to it."

"If this corn makes forty bushels to the acre, we should be able to make the payment on the mortgage and still go to Colorado to see your sister Louise," Papa promised.

The Martin farm lay in Indiana corn country, and Papa had predicted only last week that this crop would be the best in twenty years.

Papa held up his hand. "Listen! Surely I'm not hearing right. Is that hail again?"

Before anyone could say "hailstorm," the hail was pounding on the house, this time from the south instead of the west, clattering against the large windows over the window seat.

"Those south windows," Mamma shouted above the noise of the storm. "They don't have screens."

Everyone crowded over to the three windows over the window seat. One already had a crack in it.

The lights flickered, came back on, flickered, went out.

Paul's voice came from the darkness and rose above the pounding of the hail. "I guess the main line from the shed is down. I'll fix it tomorrow."

Mamma felt her way to the back porch and got the kerosene lamp from the high shelf. Soon she returned to the dining room in the circle of its yellow glow.

The hail seemed to last forever. The Martins stood by the south windows, helpless to do anything. Silently they listened and watched, peering out into the blackness, trying to find an end to the storm.

At last the roar of the hail lessened and then dropped to an occasional rattle. A steady rain continued. The Martins relaxed then and examined the windows. Several of the panes were cracked but not shattered.

There seemed nothing to do now but to sit down and wonder.

"I wonder what the crops look like," Paul said.

"I wonder if there is anything left in the garden," Mamma said.

Arnold put on his slicker and went outside. He came back shortly with a piece of ice the size of an egg.

"The garden looks pretty flat," he reported.

"Well, I doubt if I make any money by farming this year," Paul remarked as he sat down to finish his letter.

"No money, no Mary," Arnold said quietly to Janie, but Martha overheard him.

They all sat silent for a while. Martha wondered what everyone else was thinking. She herself didn't know how to feel or what to think.

Janie stared into the flame of the lamplight. "Where does the light go when you blow it out?" Nobody had an answer.

Papa stood up and tossed Janie onto his shoulder. "Well, let's go to bed, everybody. There's nothing we can do tonight. We'll look at things in the morning."

Before Martha fell asleep, she listened to the murmur of her parents' voices in the next room. She knew that they must be talking about the hailstorm. Of course, if the crops were ruined, there would be no money.

"Maybe we will have to live on beans and biscuits, like the pioneers," she thought. The idea did not frighten her very much. She loved beans, and biscuits were good if you had lots of jelly for them.

What did bother her was Arnold's remark about "no money, no Mary." Wouldn't Mary have Paul if he didn't have any money? One thing Martha dreamed about was having Mary Miller for a sister-in-law.

"I'll just die if they don't get married," she vowed.

The last thought that crossed her mind had to do with Stefana. Had the hail hit the Baronski farm? If it had, would the Baronskis move? Martha rejoiced for a moment at the possibility, but then her conscience said, "Shame, Martha, to wish bad luck on anyone, even Stefana Baronski!"

Suddenly it was morning and Janie was shaking her. "Let's get up and eat breakfast with the rest of the family. I want to see if there are any hailstones left."

CHAPTER 3

Wednesday, July 12
PAPA HAS A PLAN

WHEN MARTHA and Janie joined the rest of the family for breakfast, there was only one topic of conversation.

"Were the cows hurt by the hail?" Arnold asked. He had been allowed to sleep late because Papa knew that they would not be able to plow corn for a long time.

"No. They crowded around the north side of the straw stack and protected themselves," Papa assured him.

"Paint's off on the south side of all the buildings," Paul offered.

Mamma had been as far as the garden. "The vegetables are all pounded into the ground. Even the spirea lost all its leaves."

Martha asked, "Did the hail hit only our farm? Did the Baronskis have any?"

John Good, a neighbor to the north, had stopped by to talk to Papa. Mr. Good had heard over the radio that the hail had cut a path about three quarters of a mile wide and about ten miles long, moving from the southwest. He had been driving around to look over the hail damage. The east corner of the Good farm had been hit. No, the Baronski farm had not been touched.

"Our farm just happened to be in the direct path of the

storm. Most of the other farms were half hit or maybe hit only on the corners," Papa told the family.

When breakfast was over, Papa called for the Bible. Usually he read the Scripture suggested by the Sunday-school quarterly for morning devotions; today, however, he chose the Forty-sixth Psalm.

God is our refuge and strength, a very present help in trouble.

Therefore will not we fear, though the earth be removed, and though the mountains be carried into the midst of the sea;

Though the waters thereof roar and be troubled, though the mountains shake with the swelling thereof.

Papa's prayer for courage and help in time of trouble brought tears to Martha's eyes. She saw her mother wipe her eyes on her apron. Mamma did not often have tears.

Papa pushed his chair back from the table. "Let's go look at the hail damage." Mamma started stacking plates. "Come on, Mattie. The dishes can wait. Go get the car, Paul. We'll all go."

So everyone climbed into the car for a drive around the farm. Just as the car started through the gate, Trixie, the rat terrier, came tearing along from the barn. They waited for her and she hopped in the back. Then they drove from field to field, stopping now and then to look closely at a ruined field of corn.

Even though the sun was hot, they found little heaps of hail in protected places. Arnold filled a gunny sack and put it in the trunk of the car. When they got back to the farm-yard, he put the ice in the cool milkhouse. "Iced lemonade for supper," he said to Mamma.

They all sat down on the back steps of the house or on the swing nearby. Nobody felt like going to work. Or perhaps they could think of nothing to work at. Martha was not at a loss for words. She wanted to say, "My, isn't it terrible? Whatever will we do?" but she didn't say anything.

"The south forty is a total loss. That corn won't come out of it," Mr. Martin said. "Do you think you will get anything from your forty, Paul?"

"Only on the northwest. I might as well plow up the other two thirds of the field."

"I guess we will have to plow under the wheat, too. That twenty acres of oats on the east end looks fairly good, though. It was on the edge of the storm," Papa said.

Mamma had tears in her voice. "Those nice soybeans are a total loss." All that was left of the beans were the two-inch stems sticking out of the ground.

Then Papa said, "One thing is sure. We won't have any income from crops. We will still have our milk checks, but we will have to buy feed for the cows."

"Will we be poor?" Martha asked.

"We will have enough to eat. But we will have to be careful how we spend our money. No new clothes we don't absolutely have to have. Nothing new for the house."

"What about the mortgage?" Mamma asked.

"That $500 has to be paid to the bank in the fall. We have to scrape that mortgage money together to make our payment on the farm." He didn't say, "Or lose the farm," but Martha had heard enough about mortgages to know that when payments were not made, "they" took the farm away. She wasn't sure who "they" were.

Mamma was plainly discouraged. "I guess this is the worst summer we have had since we moved to Indiana. Even when we were drowned out, we had some kind of crop."

Papa scratched Trixie's ear. "We have been drowned out and dried out and eaten out by chinch bugs. I just never thought about hail."

Martha had never seen her parents look so beaten. "Why, they look like tired, old people," she thought with shock.

But at that moment Mamma's mood changed. She said briskly, "Well, now. Maybe we can cut down on our expenses. I think we can do without the telephone."

Everyone agreed. "Arnold can run errands in the car," Papa said.

Arnold's face lighted up. "Oh, boy! That suits me. But I suppose our trip to Colorado is off."

All the Martins looked at Mamma. They knew how very much she wanted to visit her sister Louise, whom she had not seen for fifteen years.

Mamma said quickly, "I did want to see Louise and my Aunt Sue. But of course we can't do a big thing like that this year. We have waited this long; we can wait another year."

Martha was shocked. No trip to Colorado! Nothing to look forward to. She didn't say anything, but surely Papa would not agree.

Papa agreed. "No trip to Colorado. This year we will just have to settle for a picnic at Lake Michigan and let it go at that."

Martha had an idea for saving money. "I think I should give up my piano lessons. After all, I don't need them."

But her father only smiled. "Oh, now, I wouldn't want you to make such a great sacrifice. I think we can manage to find fifty cents a week for them." Martha did not understand why piano lessons were more important than a trip to Colorado.

Arnold had been thinking. "If we plow up all that acreage, what will we plant? It is too late for corn."

Nobody had an answer. They knew that corn planted in late July could never ripen before frost.

Paul said, "We could plant some corn for silage. If frost holds off until late, it would be pretty good feed."

Mr. Martin nodded but did not answer. The family all looked to him, waiting to be told what to do, where to go from there.

Suddenly Papa stood up. "Come on, Mattie, We are going to Lake City. Paul just gave me an idea. There might be something we can do about this hailstorm."

He kissed Janie on the ear; then he kissed Martha on the ear. They squealed and shooed him away. Papa did not tease

3

often, and they loved to have him tease. For good measure, he kissed Mamma on the ear. She said, "Go along with you." But the girls could tell that she was not cross.

"Can we go to town, too?" Janie asked.

"This will be a party just for Mamma and me. No children along this time. Martha, can you get dinner for Janie and the boys?"

"Sure I can. I can cook." It occurred to Martha that Papa was doing this to cheer Mamma so that she wouldn't feel so discouraged about the crop failure.

Paul said, "Well, I guess I had better start on that wiring job. We might want to use the lights tonight," and off he went toward the barn.

Arnold stood up with a start. "Say, I forgot all about Rosebud this morning. I'll bet she is hungry." He ran for the calf shed.

When her father and mother came downstairs dressed for town, Martha thought they looked nice. Mamma wore her Sunday black-and-white print. Although Mamma was a big woman, bigger than Papa really, she looked neat and pretty when she dressed up. Her black hair was combed back into a bun and her dark eyes sparkled. Martha could not remember when her parents had gone somewhere together without one of the children along, and obviously Mamma was looking forward to the trip to town.

As for Papa, he had on his town suit and a fresh shave. Papa always said that a man should be ashamed to go to town wearing his everyday work clothes and a week's growth of beard. Martha thought he looked nice. His hair was getting very thin on top; but when he put his hat on, he looked young and handsome.

Mamma said just before she got into the car, "Now you girls finish the dishes and sweep a little. You can open a can of pork tenderloin for dinner and use anything you want from the garden."

"But, Mamma," Martha said, "we don't have a garden any more."

Mamma lost her cheerful look and sighed. "That's right. Well, open any of the canned things you need."

Before the Martins started the car, Arnold burst from the door to the calf shed and came running to them.

"Pa! My calf is gone."

Mr. Martin took his hand from the ignition. "Did you look for her? Maybe she got out and is with the cows in the back lot."

Arnold shook his head. "I looked there. I looked everywhere. She just isn't around anyplace." For all his sixteen years, he was close to tears.

Papa sat and thought for a moment. "Well, I'm sure she'll turn up someplace. You and Paul look for her while we are gone."

The Martins drove off to town. Arnold hurried back to the barn, and Martha and Janie returned to the housework assignments Mamma had given them.

Paul and Arnold came into the kitchen just as they were putting away the broom and dustpan.

"We are going to take the truck and go ask the neighbors if they have seen Rosebud," Paul said. "Want to come along?"

"No, thank you," Martha answered. "I'm too busy."

"I thought she wanted to go every time the car went," Arnold muttered to Paul as they started off with Janie.

The minute the truck motor started, Trixie appeared and demanded a ride. Trixie, the rat terrier, could smell a ride better than she could smell a rat. This dog was descended from a long line of rat terriers, all named Trixie and all white with black markings, all stub-tailed. The Trixie of this generation would be remembered as the dog who loved to ride.

Martha would have gone if she had been sure that they were not planning to stop at the Baronskis. She did not want to meet Stefana, who probably did not want to meet her. Martha was making every effort to keep her path from crossing Stefana's.

Paul and Arnold were back in an hour. They had driven around the mile square, stopping at all the neighbors to inquire about Rosebud. Nobody had seen a little fawn-colored Brown Swiss calf.

Martha followed Arnold to the horse barn to ask for further details. "What did the Baronski boys say?"

"We talked to Thaddeus, the older one. He said they hadn't seen a stray calf. Then he said something in Polish to his brother. I wonder what he said." Arnold shook a forkful of straw into the manger for Pet and Bess.

"Did you see Stefana?"

"No," he said glumly. "Now scat back to the house and fix us some dinner. I have enough to think about without listening to your chatter."

Martha scatted, and by dinnertime had her meal on the table. The boys ate with a good appetite, and Paul said, "Good dinner," as he got up to go back to work.

"You're learning," Arnold admitted. "What was wrong with that corn bread?"

"Nothing!" Martha exclaimed and started stacking dishes. "I just forgot the salt." How mean of him to have noticed such a little, insignificant detail!

About the middle of the afternoon, Martha and Janie stationed themselves at the mailbox so that they could see the Martin car when it turned at the bridge. They lay on their backs in the hail-flattened grass and watched a white cloud drift after another white cloud, "playing tag slowly," as Janie remarked. A robin perched on a nearby fence post.

"Why do they call you robin redbreast? You are an orangy brown," Janie commented. The robin, annoyed that she had criticized him, flew away. "I didn't mean to hurt your feelings," she called after him.

They saw a car coming down the road; so they jumped up to thumb a ride from the mailbox into the barnyard. Then they jumped back into the grass in confusion, for they realized that this was not their parents' car. The Baronskis drove slowly by. Two men were in the front seat.

They watched the car turn into their own gate. The brothers drove behind the barn out of sight.

"Those are Stefana's brothers," Martha whispered to Janie, even though the Baronskis were now out of earshot. "What do they want here?"

Janie's eyes widened. "Are they bad men?" she whispered back.

Martha did not know if they were or not. "Well, I just don't want them hanging around here," she said.

"Prob'ly returning the pitchfork," Janie said reasonably. Then she changed the subject. "Marty, what's a morgeege? Papa said we had to pay the morgeege."

"It's the money we owe on the farm. Papa couldn't pay for the farm all at one time when he bought it."

Martha had never before been concerned about the mortgage. She had heard Papa tell Mamma the news that some neighbor "couldn't pay his mortgage; so he lost the farm." And he and Mamma would look at each other anxiously. Then Papa would always brighten and say, "But things look pretty good for us this year." Martha wondered what Papa's plan was for solving the hailstorm problem.

The Baronski brothers drove out of the yard and went on east. Martha and Janie watched the car disappear in the distance, and did not notice another car that came from the west until it was almost upon them.

"Anybody want a ride?" Papa called. They hopped in for the short ride into the barnyard. Paul and Arnold came from the barns when their father honked the horn. It seemed as though everyone expected something special to come of this trip to town.

"What did you bring us?" Janie asked.

"Look in the grocery sack," Mamma said. "Even though we were down to our last dime, your father would bring you a sack of candy from town." In spite of her words, her tone was cheerful.

Janie dived into the sack and came forth with a bag of caramels.

Paul asked, "Well, what did you find out?"

"I went to the county agent's office and he gave me an idee. I have something to show you." Papa got out and opened the trunk of the car. The family crowded around expectantly, waiting to see the miracle that would solve all their problems. Martha saw two uninteresting burlap sacks bulging with something.

"We hope that this, by fall, will be the payment on our farm," Papa said. He opened a sack and took a handful of seed to show them. It was like no grain that Martha had ever seen. Each kernel was three-sided, like a beechnut.

"Some new kind of wheat?" Paul asked.

"No, it isn't new and it really isn't a wheat, but it is called buckwheat."

"You mean like in buckwheat pancakes?" Martha asked skeptically.

"Exactly," Mamma said. "We are going to raise enough buckwheat for a million pancakes."

"I think we can plant at least forty acres. If you want to, Paul, you can put some in, too."

Paul did not look convinced. "This is the middle of July. When will it be ripe?"

"The county agent said it will take eight or ten weeks to mature. That gives us until the middle of September. We seldom have a killing frost before then. Of course, we will have to work fast to get it in the ground as soon as possible. But I think this is the only answer to the hailstorm."

"Well, if you and the county agent think we should chance it, I'm willing to try. I believe I could get a few hours of plowing in yet this afternoon."

Paul headed for the tractor and Mamma and Janie took the groceries to the house. Arnold had forgotten his worries in the excitement, but now he remembered.

"Papa, we can't find the calf anywhere. Do you suppose somebody took her?"

Papa stopped tugging at the sack of buckwheat. "She isn't with the cows? Or along the road?"

"Paul and I took the truck and looked for her. Anyway, how could she have got out? I latched the barn door."

"Did you fasten it on the outside as well as on the inside?" Rosebud had grown so smart that she could open the latch with her nose, Martha knew.

Arnold's face went blank. "No. I didn't hook the door on the outside. I forgot that Rosebud can open the door herself. But even if she did get out, where is she now? I think she wandered out on the road and somebody picked her up."

"That could happen, I suppose," Papa hesitated.

"The Baronskis were here in their old car this afternoon," Martha offered.

Arnold accepted the idea quickly. "That older Baronski! I'll bet Thaddeus picked her up either last night or this morning."

"Prob'ly plans to sell her," Martha added.

"He saw her yesterday when he got the pitchfork from the calf shed. Decided right then to help himself," Arnold said bitterly.

"Now don't jump to conclusions like that," Papa warned. "All we can do is wait to see if Rosebud turns up."

There seemed nothing more to be said, and so Arnold went back to the barn and Mr. Martin went to change into his work clothes.

Martha went to find Janie and the caramels. She took seven as her share, and then when Janie was not looking, Martha slipped upstairs to deposit them in her top dresser drawer under her box of fancy handkerchiefs. They joined a pile of three kisses and two sticks of gum. Martha was saving them for later use.

She felt considerably more cheerful since her parents had come home from town. She knew that Paul, too, was hopeful about Papa's plan. But Arnold! He would not be happy until he found Rosebud. Oh, well. Maybe he deserved a little scare. He was so smart-alecky.

"I hope Rosebud doesn't turn up until tomorrow. Arnold can just stew a while," Martha said to Janie.

At suppertime, however, even Arnold cheered up. After the main part of the meal, Paul said, "Let me get the dessert." He left the table and went outside.

"Now what is he going to do?" Mamma asked. "We are having canned peaches for dessert."

"Arnie made—" Janie began, but Martha clapped her hand over Janie's mouth to keep her from telling the secret.

Then Paul came back from the shed with a pail.

Janie shouted, "Homemade ice cream. We made it with hailstones."

Paul dished it up with the help of the other children. They set heaping bowls before their parents. Of course, Mr. and Mrs. Martin were astonished.

"But who knew how to make it? My, but it's good!" Mamma exclaimed.

"This goes down easy. And I thought all that ice went into the lemonade," Papa said.

"Arnold cooked the custard and we all turned the freezer," Janie informed them.

"Of course, we had a hard time keeping Martha and Janie from eating the whole freezerful before you got home," Arnold said. "They kept tasting it."

Martha protested. "You are just aggravating. Who was it put the hailstones down my back?"

Later that night Papa and Mamma sat at the kitchen table figuring with pencil and paper. Martha stopped on her way to bed for a long drink of water at the kitchen sink.

"This all works out on paper," Papa said. "If the weather is with us for the rest of the summer, we ought to make ends meet." Then his shoulders sagged. "But I don't quite see how the boys and I can get all that land ready for another crop, let alone get it planted in time."

"Threshing will start pretty soon," Mamma injected.

"I wonder if John Good would rent me his tractor for a few days. The work would go lots faster with another tractor. Martha, get to bed."

Martha heard him telephoning as she went to sleep.

CHAPTER 4

Monday, July 17
COWS AND COWBOYS

THE NEXT MORNING Martha was awakened at sunup by the sound of tractors. She ran to the window and saw a line of eight men on eight tractors pulling into the barnyard.

In a moment her mother's excited voice came up the stairway. "Martha, get up! The neighbors have come in for a planting bee. My, such a surprise."

"Coming, Mamma. Wake up, Janie." Martha hurried into her clothes.

Eight men! This would be as good as threshing day. How would they feed them? Was there a Baronski in the group? Martha stood at the top of the stairs and, grasping the railing on each side, swung herself down in three long leaps.

Later Martha and Janie watched from the fence as the tractors swung around the field east of the barn. One tractor pulled a disk and behind it came a tractor pulling a harrow that smoothed out the clods. Following this one was a tractor with the drill that planted the buckwheat.

Papa came along then. "I want you girls to bridle Bessie and carry water to the men. It's awful hot out there."

Janie said, "Isn't it fun, being hailed out?"

"Fun?" Papa replied. "That's not the word I'd use."

John Good had told Mamma not to worry about feeding

the men. About eleven-thirty cars started arriving filled with women, children, and picnic baskets. They laid out the dinner in the back yard, and Mamma got to visit with women she saw only once in a while at school and church meetings or in the grocery store.

Papa said the blessing for the food, thanking God not only for the bountiful meal but for the help of good neighbors. Then everyone filled his plate and sat down on the grass to eat.

John Good had been the one who had organized the planting bee, but he refused to take any credit for it when Papa tried to thank him.

"Now, Elmer, you know as well as I do that if it had been anybody else hailed out, you would have been the first one over there to help."

Martha looked around the circle for some of the Baronski family. There was no one. They had not sent a tractor; so of course the womenfolk hadn't come for the dinner. Why not? They lived closer than any of the other families. Didn't they believe in helping their neighbors? Well, she guessed that was the kind of treatment you could expect from the Baronskis.

After the noon meal and a short rest, the men went back to the fields and the women and children packed up and drove home. The men quit working early in the evening so that they could go home to do their chores.

The Martin men worked again on Friday and Saturday, and by Saturday sundown seventy acres of buckwheat and forty acres of ensilage corn had been planted.

On Monday morning as he left the breakfast table, Papa said to Arnold, "Try to get the lawns mowed sometime today. This place is beginning to look shaggy."

There had not been much damage done to the lawn by the hail because the grass had been protected by the trees. The grass now looked long and untidy, and Papa did not like an untidy farm.

Right after she had finished breakfast dishes, Martha

rolled the lawn mower from the shed and started the job. Pushing the old mower was hard work, and Martha admitted to herself that she would not have been interested in the job if it had been assigned to her. But Martha wanted to mow the lawn, just to show the family that she could do something they didn't think she was able to do. She wondered what Arnold would say when he found she had done his chore.

When she was half finished with the front yard, she collapsed on the grass, exhausted and perspiring. She lay on her back under the crab apple tree and watched the clouds. The sky was a perfect blue. The air was perfect, just hot enough, and the smell was perfect, grassy and sweet.

"I want to remember this moment all my life. At this little space I am perfectly happy. Well, not quite. I would like to be twelve rather than eleven; I would rather have brown eyes than green eyes. But otherwise, everything is just right."

Martha got up to finish mowing the front lawn. When she was through, she put the mower away. Arnold could mow the back yard himself. It was too big for her.

Martha called to Janie, who was collecting catalpa pods for the playhouse, "Let's go ride Bessie."

"All right." Janie came running, glad to have Martha offer to play with her.

Bessie was easy to bridle, but she would not take a saddle. Everyone who rode Bessie rode bareback. The two girls climbed on and started down the road at Bessie's leisurely walk.

"Come on, we are cowboys and we want a horse that gallops," Martha urged.

But Bessie wanted to stop to nibble the grass that grew along the edge of the dirt road. The girls scolded and switched in an effort to keep her going. They went east as far as the line fence, then turned around to start home.

"Isn't that the mail lady coming 'way down there?" Janie asked.

"Hurry up, Bessie. Let's get home so we can talk to her," Martha pleaded.

"Maybe she has something for us from Sears."

"Don't be silly. We haven't ordered anything," Martha said.

She gave the pony a smart slap with the willow switch. Bessie suddenly realized that she was on the way home, and she took off for her stall at a trot that bounced the girls breathless. With another slap of the switch, she leveled off into a gallop like a real cow pony. Martha clung to her mane and Janie held tight to Martha's waist.

The pony had no intention, however, of holding a conversation with the mail lady. Bessie went through the gate without slowing up. She saw the open barn door and headed for it.

"Whoa!" Martha yelled.

And "Whoa up," Janie echoed.

But Bessie didn't whoa. She went through the open barn door, skidding to a stop that sent Martha over her head and into a pile of hay in front of the manger. Janie lost her hold on Martha's waist and slid off sideways. She settled with a plop in a corner of the stall.

They picked themselves up and scolded the pony. "You are the most obstinate, mule-headed, stubborn, balky, cantankerous pony I know," Martha said as she poured some oats into her trough.

The noon whistle in Cummings blew as the girls went for the mail. Sure enough, there was something from Sears, the big fall catalog.

When the men came in to dinner, Martha noticed that Arnold glanced at the newly mowed lawn, but said nothing.

"Isn't he even going to thank me?" she wondered.

She forgot about her good deed at the dinner table when Mr. Martin announced his good news: "The first planting of buckwheat is up!" He thought there would be a good stand.

"Do you have to plow it to keep the weeds down the way you plow corn?" Martha asked.

"No, it makes such a thick foliage that it chokes out the weeds. You just wait until it blooms! That will be a pretty sight."

After dinner, Mr. Martin gave instructions. "Arnold and Martha, I want you to herd cows this afternoon. Take them out on the road west between here and the bridge. Be sure you don't let them go beyond the bridge, hear me?"

"Why herd cows today when you have so much other work to do?" Mamma asked.

"The pasture was hurt by the hail and I don't want to let it get too short. Janie, you can help, too."

Mamma said that she would do the dishes, and the girls were happy with this arrangement. They got out to the barnyard just as Arnold was driving the thirty cows and heifers onto the road. Martha climbed up behind Arnold, who was mounted on Lady, the riding horse. Arnold lifted Janie up to sit in front of him in the saddle. They trailed the lazy cows down the road for a distance; then Arnold said, "I want to ride ahead so that they won't go past the bridge."

He gave Lady free rein and she found her way through the herd; then she broke into a trot. With every step that the horse took, Martha flew up four inches and sat down hard. Martha had not realized that the beautiful Lady had such a hard backbone.

"Don't go so fast!" she shouted. "I think I'm sitting on a rail fence." Arnold couldn't know how it felt because he was on the saddle. He kicked Lady again, and she trotted faster. With each klop, klop of Lady's hoofs on the soft sand, Martha bounced up and then down on the horse's bony back. When she thought she could not endure it for another moment, Arnold put Lady into a gallop, which was much better bump-wise. Then just as she was beginning to enjoy the ride, they arrived at the bridge and stopped.

Arnold said, "Now you girls get off here. I'm going to do some detective work. I want to ride by the Baronski pasture and see if I can see my calf."

Martha slid off Lady's tail, landing neatly on her feet,

45

and Janie scrambled down from her perch. Arnold rode off across the bridge and up the north road. To his left were the few cows belonging to the Baronskis. They were grazing in the middle of the field.

Martha looked up toward the Baronski house. She thought she saw Stefana come out of the kitchen door and sit on the porch. Martha wondered if Stefana was lonely, living there with only grownups, not even having a little sister.

Glancing again at Arnold, Martha saw that he had opened the gate and had ridden into the Baronski pasture. "I hope none of them see him and come chasing after him," Martha said.

Janie shivered. "I am on peas and noodles, I am so scared for Arnie."

Martha laughed. "You mean on pins and needles, silly."

"No, I don't. That is what the man on the radio said. He was on peas and noodles. Martha, tell me again, how does the man get into the radio?"

This was a question Martha had tried to answer many times, and because she didn't understand it very well herself, she was glad to see Arnold come galloping back.

"Did you see Rosebud?" Martha asked as he dismounted.

"Well, I didn't see anything that looked exactly like Rosebud, but there was one calf that might be mine. I'm just sure that those Baronski boys have her. I wish Pa would go ask their pa outright."

Arnold pulled a rope from his pocket and started tying knots. They all relaxed on the grass, talking of this and that.

"I like Brown Swiss cows," Janie said as she watched one of the Martin herd grazing nearby. "When I grow up, I will have a farm and I will raise cows."

"Do you want to be a farmer?" Arnold asked, surprised. "I guess it is good living if you like to take chances on the weather, like that hailstorm. Personally, I'd rather teach."

"Everybody likes Miss Williams at Indian Grove," Martha said. "She lets me read the library books during the summer."

46

"Reading is good for you. You do all the reading you can," Arnold said with brotherly approval.

At that moment Martha felt very sisterly toward Arnold. Here he was talking to them as though they were all friends, not making fun of what they said, not even reminding Martha that her reading often resulted in burned potatoes.

"Now my problem," Arnold was saying, "is getting enough money together so that I can go to college and read all the books I want to read."

Martha laughed. "I thought your only problem was learning to tie knots."

Arnold shook his head. "As soon as I learn to tie all the knots in the book, I will be through with this. You never know. My rope-tying ability may come in handy someday." Arnold always said that about any project he undertook, whether it was lily pool construction or a course in muscle building.

Arnold happened to glance up the road. He jumped to his feet. "Martha! You've let the cows go past the bridge and they are in Paul's cornfield. Come on. Help me get them out."

"What do you mean *I* let them go into the cornfield?" Martha demanded, forgetting any sisterly feelings she had toward Arnold.

Arnold was running toward the hole in the fence. "Don't argue. Chase!"

The field Paul rented had a poor fence along the road. For this reason Arnold had been warned not to let the cows go beyond the bridge. Five cows had found a weak place in the fence and had plunged into the field for a delectable meal. Arnold and Martha tried to round them up and to get them out of the cornfield while Janie stood watch on the road. But the cows had other ideas.

"Hey, Queenie," Arnold pleaded as he eased a cow up to the break in the fence. "Come now, just go out the same way you came in."

But just as the cow seemed to be going out of the field

47

through the opening, she would break-and run in another direction.

"Stupid cow!" Martha yelled at Beauty as she did the same thing.

"Stupid-hupid cow," Janie shouted to a cow still on the road. She hit one over the nose with a stick as it tried to join its sisters in the cornfield.

Arnold and Martha seemed to be making no progress in getting the cows out of the corn. The five cows were still in there and Janie was about to lose her battle with the rest of the herd.

At that moment help arrived from two directions. From the east Trixie came running full speed, somehow having sensed that she was missing out on the excitement. From the west a large, bushy-haired man rode up on a black plow horse.

The older Baronski brother joined the battle of thirty cows against two small girls and a boy. He yelled at them in Polish and flourished a willow switch so that it whistled. For a moment Martha wondered on whose side of the battle he was, but he soon proved that he was for people and against cows, anyway against cows in cornfields.

By much whooping and hollering, chasing and switching, barking and yipping, they got the five cows out of the corn without very much damage to the crop.

"Thanks, Thaddeus," Arnold called after him as he rode back across the bridge on his plow horse. "Thanks a lot."

Thaddeus smiled and waved.

By then it was time to get the cows back home. "Want to ride back?" Arnold asked the girls.

"I won't ride with someone who accuses me of letting the cows get in the corn when his father distinctly told him to watch them. No, thanks," Martha said with great dignity.

Janie said she would walk with Martha.

"Well, O.K. I have to get home and get these cows milked so that I have time to mow the back yard before supper. Lucky for me that somebody has already mowed the front." He gave Lady a slap and galloped off after the cows.

Martha said to Janie, "I can't figure it out."

"You mean you can't figure out who mowed the lawn? Why, you did!"

"No, I can't figure it out. He may be in trouble with the law. He stole Arnold's calf. He wouldn't come to our planting bee. And still he helped us get those cows out of the corn."

How could one person be both good and bad?

4

CHAPTER 5

Friday, July 21
THRESHING DAY

"I DON'T THINK we have ever put in such a busy summer," Papa said Tuesday at breakfast.

"We have never been hailed out before," Mamma reminded him.

She had been helping more with the milking and other chores. Sometimes she and Arnold did the evening chores alone while the men worked past dark in the fields.

"Today I could use six boys and three tractors. Paul can ride the binder while Arnold drives the tractor and we will get that oats cut. I'll do the shocking. We just have to get done because they want to start threshing tomorrow," Papa said.

"I will help shock this time," Mamma offered.

"Pshaw, you don't have to. We'll manage," Papa protested.

"I used to before the boys were big enough to help. That twenty acres of oats is so thin that it shouldn't take us long. Martha, you can get dinner."

"Janie, you can help, too. You trot around with the water jugs so we won't get too thirsty." So Papa gave everyone an assignment for the day.

At noon Martha asked at the dinner table, "Why are you

going threshing this summer? I didn't think you would since we don't have much to thresh."

"We have only twenty acres right now, but I want the crew to do my buckwheat when it is ready in the fall. So I will have to help now and send another man, too," her father explained.

Arnold brought up the problem of his college education. "I just have to find that calf or I won't have a money-making project this summer. How can I go to college without money? You want me to go to college, don't you?"

"My, yes," Mamma assured him. "I have more education than your pa, and I think it always helps me to get the best of him."

"Pshaw," Papa said mildly. "You finished the sixth grade and I got half way through the fifth. Funny I never noticed that you were so much smarter than me."

" 'Smarter than I,' " Mamma corrected. "Anyway I learned more grammar than you did."

Martha decided that her parents must be in pretty good spirits if they could tease each other again.

Arnold brought the conversation back to the present. "Do you know what I heard in town yesterday? Ben Yoder told me that the reason the Baronskis moved out here was because one of the boys got into trouble with the police in Gary. Ben used to work in the mills, you know."

This was startling news to Martha. Probably those boys had stolen things in Gary, too.

Mr. Martin didn't look surprised. "Yes, I heard that, too, when they first moved here. That doesn't mean that they are going to get into trouble here, though." Obviously, he considered the subject closed.

After dinner, Martha joined Paul and Arnold as they were resting a few minutes in the back yard before returning to the oats field. Arnold was reading *Ivanhoe* and he was reluctant to put the book aside and get back on his tractor.

"Just wait until I finish this chapter?" he asked.

"How long is it?"

"About twenty pages." He grinned. "I just started a new one." Arnold threw the book to Martha and gave a long stretch.

Paul said, "That reminds me. What did you do the other day when you were supposed to be plowing with Pet and Bess? I came in for gas for the tractor and during that time you didn't get any plowing done."

Arnold's face grew red and he said uncomfortably, "The horses need a rest once in a while, you know."

Paul looked at him closely and then got up. "Let's get back to the field."

On Wednesday Paul and Mr. Martin started the rounds with the threshing crew. They were gone from early in the morning until evening, when they came rattling home on the hayrack. Even after a long day of threshing, Pet and Bess would come through the gate at a fast trot, always threatening the gate post.

Papa announced on Wednesday evening: "We are to have threshers Friday. I'm afraid you will have to get dinner, even though it won't take long to do ours."

Mamma said, "All right. Arnold can go tomorrow and ask Kate Birky and Mrs. Yoder if they can help me." Arnold had the privilege of running the errands now that the Martins had no telephone.

"Should you offer to help Mrs. Baronski? The threshers will be there on Saturday," Papa said.

The next day Arnold stopped at the Baronski place on his way home from the Birkys. Mrs. Baronski thanked him for Mamma's offer, but she said her sister from Gary was staying with her and would help with the cooking. She would not need Mamma's help. Martha was relieved. If Mamma had had to go to the Baronskis, she would have expected Martha to go along to play with Stefana. What an embarrassment that would have been!

Friday was a day to look forward to. Delcie Birky would come with her mother and the two girls would have all day to play. It was unfortunate that the Birkys, with all their ten children, did not have a girl Janie's age. As it was, Janie would have to tag along with Martha and Delcie.

Delcie, in spite of her delicate-sounding name, was quite a tomboy. Although on Sunday she would appear in church looking quite ladylike in her older sister's outgrown dress, on any weekday she was ready for action in her older brother's outgrown overalls. The sad fact about Delcie was that she lived too far away to be of any use as a bosom friend.

"I hope it doesn't rain and spoil things," Martha thought. How disappointing if the Martins would *not* have to feed the threshers.

Early Friday morning Arnold went to Cummings, about five miles away, for groceries. He brought home a large beef roast. Beef was a luxury, fed only to threshers and Sunday company. Also for the occasion Arnold bought a chunk of ice for the icebox on the back porch. There would be iced lemonade for dinner. Threshers expected a good meal, for they worked very hard. Mamma wanted to be sure that when they went home to their wives in the evening, they would report that the food had been good.

Kate and Delcie and Howie Birky arrived about eight o'clock.

Delcie was a startling sight in a bright blue satin dress. Martha stared at her cousin, having expected the usual overall-clad tomboy. The dress she was wearing was obviously meant for a girl ten years older. It clung to her slender body and then ended in a wide ruffle that extended from her knees almost to her ankles. She was, as usual, barefooted.

"How do you like it?" Delcie asked, turning around slowly, one arm akimbo and the other held aloft to show the graceful flare of the cape sleeve.

"Oh, it's george-ous," Janie said.

"Gorgeous," corrected Martha. "Yes, it really is," she agreed, almost enviously. "Where did you get it?"

"Oh, the Hansons sent us a box of clothes yesterday and this was in it. Mamma hasn't had time yet to take up the hem."

Lucky Delcie! Because they were a large family, the Birkys often got the outgrown clothes from their Chicago relatives.

"I just had to wear it today. It's a bit tight around the knees. I won't be able to play any running games. It's a pretty color, don't you think?"

The blue of the dress matched her eyes and was very becoming to her fair skin and hair. But then, Delcie was a curly-haired beauty, no matter what she wore. Anyway, that was Mamma's opinion.

Martha looked down at her bare knees, which were two inches below the hem of her skirt. She was wearing last year's school dress, and she had plainly outgrown it.

For the time being, however, the girls had to forget about their clothes and make themselves useful at a few chores. The girls would be expected to help a little, but then they would be free most of the day. They were given the job of cutting up apples for sauce. The Birkys had brought a bushel, knowing that the Martin apples had all been knocked off by the hail.

Kate started on the pies, lemon and chocolate. "Make five," Mamma said. Just the idea of those pies made Martha's mouth water.

"How many men are in the crew this year?" Kate asked.

"Sixteen, counting Arnold and Howie. And I can get only twelve up to my table," Mamma lamented. She hated to have men waiting to eat at a second table.

"Why don't you put that table you have on the porch at the end of your dining table? Let the men sit on the window seat at this end and on the piano bench at that end. Then you can seat fourteen. Arnold and Howie can eat with us." Kate was used to feeding large numbers.

Mrs. Yoder arrived about this time and was given the job of peeling potatoes. The women enjoyed working together and talking. Martha would have liked to stay to hear the talk, but she and Delcie were told to set the table.

Their next task was to fix a place outside the back door

for the men to wash. They set up two orange crates with wash basins and filled the boiler with water. Soap, mirrors, and combs were laid out. They hung the towels on the fence, but not the best towels. Everybody knew how dirty the men got when they threshed.

"Threshers get the towels black as coal," Martha said.

"Threshing dust is not black as coal. It is more yellow," Janie corrected her.

"I was just aggravating," Martha said.

"I am going to tell Mamma that you are always aggravating," Janie threatened.

"Oh, don't be such a blabber mouth."

"Blabber mouse?" Janie asked, her attention caught by the new word.

"Blabber mouth," Martha corrected.

"Oh, blabber mouth."

When the girls' chores were finished, they went out behind the sand hill where the crew was threshing. There they found a confusion of busy men, dust, and noise. Two men were tossing bundles of oats into the maw of the thresher. The oats came out one spout into a wagon where Arnold was on duty to see that the wagon filled properly. Papa was on top of the straw stack guiding another long funnel so that the straw would stack neatly. He was covered with dust. The air had a threshing-day smell of dry, powdery chaff.

Howie, Delcie's brother, was the official water boy, carrying the jugs out to the men in the field. When he returned to the milkhouse to refill his jugs, the girls proposed to help him, but Howie was plainly ungrateful.

Delcie and Martha saw that Paul was ready to leave for the oats field; giving Janie the slip, they climbed aboard his empty hayrack for the ride. Delcie had some difficulty hitching up her satin dress so that she could take the big step up to the tongue of the rack and then over the end of the rack.

Pet and Bess took off as though they had been dynamited, and the girls who had been standing up at one moment were sitting down the next. They then bounced up and down and around on the hard planks of the rack bed as the horses dashed out to the field.

Paul pulled up to a waiting pitcher, and he began to toss the bundles up onto the rack. The girls offered to help Paul stack the bundles, but he refused their offer.

"You can help best by staying out of my way," he said firmly.

While Paul loaded his rack, the girls wandered over to the ditch that separated the oats field from the buckwheat field that Paul was farming. Willows had grown up on both sides of the ditch. They were taller than the girls' heads and in this particular spot had not been damaged by the hail.

"Look, Delcie," Martha called. "Here is a little path leading into the willows. Let's see where it goes."

Delcie followed as Martha pushed into a narrow opening that led through a dense thicket. They came out into a small, grassy open place and stood in a shady little room surrounded by the leafy green of the willows.

"Why, it's a hide-out," Delcie said. "Isn't it cozy?"

The girls lay on their backs in the soft grass in a little world of their own. All the sounds that reached them were gentle and far away. A bird tittered and insects buzzed someplace in the willows. The distance reduced the roar and clatter of the threshing machine to an irregular hum.

"Isn't it peaceful?" Delcie and Martha spoke in one voice. Without speaking another word they hooked little fingers and carried out the ritual for making a wish after saying the same thing at the same time. After each had silently made her wish, they nodded at each other.

"Needles," Martha said.

"Pins," Delcie answered.

"Shakespeare."

"Twins." Then they released little fingers.

Far away they heard a shrill call: "Stefana," and the answer, "Yes, Mamma."

"We aren't far from Baronskis, you know," Martha said.

"How are you and Stefana getting along? Have you

56

made friends with her?" Delcie asked. Martha had told her earlier in the summer of her feelings about Stefana.

"Oh, we haven't seen each other all summer. I still hate and despise her. She thinks she is so smart." Even as she said it, Martha's conscience bothered her. Was that one of the Ten Commandments: "Thou shalt not hate"?

To change the subject, Martha said, "Did the willows grow like this, or did someone cut an opening? I don't see any cut stumps."

"Look at this!" Delcie held up a short length of rope. "It looks like something you would tie a horse with."

Martha had a sudden idea. "Or a calf!" She looked around more carefully. "Do you suppose the Baronski boys used this for a hiding place for Rosebud?"

Delcie said, "They could have. You said we aren't far from their place."

Suddenly the cozy little hide-out became dark and scary. The girls by common agreement crept out through the narrow tunnel into the sunlight and ran for Paul's hayrack.

Paul had finished loading the rack, and they climbed on for the ride back to the threshing machine. This was one of the best parts of the day. The girls lay on their backs in a hollow on the very top of the load, and they floated home on a high sea of oats bundles. All they could see was the blue sky above them and the prickly bundles of straw around them. The sounds of the creaking wagon and the rattle of the harness were muffled by distance.

"You know we are in great danger," Delcie observed solemnly.

"Why?" asked Martha, her skin beginning to prickle with goose bumps.

"This load may tip over. When we go around a corner, you know. It happens all the time."

"Wouldn't that be thrilling!" Martha sat upright and forgot about her goose bumps. "An oats-bundle burial. When they would dig us out, they would find us pale, lovely, and dead."

"Oh, I doubt it. My brother Howie was covered with a rackful of bundles once, at the very bottom. He just clawed himself out."

"Oh, well—Howie," said Martha, dismissing him lightly. Howie was notorious for his death-defying escapades. "I would enjoy being tipped over."

"Let's go talk to Paul," Delcie suggested; so they crawled forward to where Paul was seated in his own nest on the edge of the load. He was holding the reins loosely, letting Pet and Bess step along steadily with their high-piled wagon.

"We want to know what you are dreaming about," Martha said, speaking to the back of his right ear.

"About Mary Miller, I bet," Delcie offered to the left ear.

It was evident that Paul was caught off guard. He jumped a little, half turned around. "What do you mean, scaring me like that." It was evident, too, that he must have been thinking about Mary, for his tan became flushed.

The horses, without lessening their pace, started to pull the wagon around a narrow corner. The wagon scraped against a gate post; and Paul, realizing that he should have slowed the horses down to ease the top-heavy load through the gate, pulled on the reins and shouted a loud "Whoa, there!"

But he was too late. With a loud creak, the wagon shifted and the bundles began to slide. Martha felt herself floating, slowly as in a dream, toward her oats-bundle burial. She had no time to think of herself as dead and lovely, for suddenly the ride was over and she was sliding down a pile of bundles into the thick dust of the lane.

A bright blue bundle followed her. Delcie, helpless in her blue satin skirt, landed on Martha's stomach. Without saying a word, the girls picked themselves up and looked for Paul. He was perched atop the overturned wagon, clinging to one of the front posts of the rack.

Paul looked at them, and for a minute Martha thought he was going to explode. But he didn't. He merely said,

"You girls hike up to the thresher and tell Arnold to come help me get this loaded again. The other wagons have to go through this gate."

They hiked. Delcie tried to hurry in her tight skirt with the blue ruffle flying around her ankles, and she took very short, very fast steps. Little puffs of dust chased the girls' scampering feet.

When they told Arnold of Paul's difficulty, without mentioning their own responsibility for it, he grabbed a pitchfork and rushed to his brother's rescue.

"Let's not go back to the field," Martha said sensibly as they watched him dash off.

"It's dinnertime anyway," Delcie agreed.

The dragonlike threshing machine coughed and stopped. The men tied their teams in the shade and let them eat their oats from the boxes on the back of the hayracks.

The men trooped into the back yard to wash up.

Martha and Delcie helped in the kitchen, running errands, filling glasses with lemonade, setting the chairs around the table.

They could hear the sounds of splashing and sudsing and sputtering as the men scrubbed their faces and necks and arms. There was talk and laughter as they taunted and teased each other about being lazy or slow or awkward. It seemed that Thaddeus Baronski had the championship for stacking the most bundles on a load. When Paul finally appeared, they teased him about his upset wagon.

After the men had washed up, they went around the house to the front yard. When Papa announced that dinner was ready, they filed through the front door and took their places at the long table.

Papa said grace and they started to eat. There was no more loud laughter and only enough talk to get the food around the table. Eating was serious business. Martha refilled lemonade glasses, refilled the bread plate, carried in refills of all the dishes. The women passed the pie and poured more lemonade. The meal was over in twenty minutes.

Martha had had the opportunity during the meal to take a good look at Thaddeus and Casimir Baronski. They looked quite a bit alike, with brown, longish hair and even features. Martha thought she saw something wild and strange about them. As they left the table, they spoke to each other in Polish. Martha wondered what they were talking about that they didn't want the other men to understand. Were they talking about Rosebud?

After the men had filed out into the front yard again, it was time to feed the hungry women, the starving girls, and the famished boys. Kate Birky and Mrs. Yoder cleared the table and reset it. Mamma filled the bowls and set the pitcher of lemonade on the table. Then they all sat down to a leisurely meal.

The threshing crew finished shortly after dinner and left for the Baronski farm.

"I guess they will be back in another two months or so. Then we will feed them for three or four days," Mamma said.

She was thinking of the buckwheat that she hoped would make a crop worth threshing. Of course, at this moment, the buckwheat was hardly out of the ground. Martha wondered how it could possibly grow fast enough to be ready to thresh before winter.

"Let's go play in your playhouse," Delcie suggested.

Giving Janie the slip again, they left the house for the playhouse on the sand hill. Mamma did not even call them back to help with the dishes.

"That hide-out in the willows would make a nice playhouse if it were not so far away," Martha said as they rearranged their kitchen.

"Let's go back there and take another look at that hide-out," Delcie said. "We could look around, maybe find some other rooms like that one."

The two girls walked out to the oats field. The field had a strange appearance now that all the oats shocks were gone and the men, horses, and wagons had moved out. The field lay flat and level, the stubble crisscrossed by wagon tracks.

Martha grabbed Delcie's arm and pointed across the field in the direction of the hide-out. A man walked into the opening and disappeared into the willows.

"Who was that?" Delcie whispered, although they were too far away for anyone to have heard.

"I don't know," Martha whispered back. "I didn't get a good look."

The girls sat down at the edge of the field to watch. Nothing happened. No one came out of the hide-out and no one went in. But the girls were not brave enough to go over to investigate.

Finally Delcie said, "I had better go home. My mother will want to leave pretty soon."

As they walked back to the Martin house, they tried to decide whom they had seen.

"It could be only one of the Baronskis," Martha concluded. "They are still using that hide-out for something."

"Delcie. Del—cie!" A shrill call came from the house. Both girls started running, although Delcie could take only short steps in her tight dress. When they reached the house, they found that Delcie's mother was ready to go home; so the girls had no further opportunity to discuss the mysterious hide-out.

That evening when Arnold started upstairs for bed, Martha cornered him at the bottom of the stairway.

"Me and Delcie—"

"Delcie and I!" Arnold corrected her wearily.

"Me and Delcie," Martha repeated firmly, "found a little clearing in the willows where we think the Baronskis hid the calf."

"Oh, you did?" Arnold sounded half interested.

"And then this afternoon when we went back we saw somebody go into the hide-out. We were sort of scared. Do you think it was one of the Baronskis?"

"Could have been. You'd better stay away from that hide-out and not get into any trouble." Arnold pushed past her and went upstairs. Martha stared after him in surprise.

He was a hard one to figure out. Martha had thought he would jump with excitement when she told him about the hide-out. Oh, well. She would find that calf by herself. That would show him.

CHAPTER 6

Saturday, July 22
MARTHA IMPRESSES
THE FAMILY

THE EXCITEMENT of threshing day was over. The day after was by contrast very boring. Because she had nothing else to do, Martha wandered out to the playhouse on the sand hill. Locust and catalpa trees grew around the edge of the hill, making a cool corner. The sand was pleasant, almost moist under her bare feet. Narrow boards had been laid out to form the rooms of the playhouse. A cement block made a cupboard, and a good cardboard box was used as a table.

Janie joined her and they gathered food for the cupboard. Dog fennel blossoms made good fried eggs with their daisy-like yellow centers and white edges.

"But they are so tiny. Eggs are much, much bigger." Janie liked her things to be exact.

"Don't be so particular. Here are some green beans to go with the eggs." Martha produced some catalpa pods, all of them a foot long.

"Green beans just don't grow that big. If they did, they would be too long for my stomach," Janie complained.

"Oh, well. Let's do something else." As usual, Martha found that it was more fun to organize a playhouse than to play in it.

"We just were ready to start playing," Janie wailed. She

stayed to play by herself, but Martha went to sit on the porch steps.

Why play at cooking? Maybe she should ask her mother if she could make something for dinner. With her elbows on her knees and her chin in her hands, Martha went off into one of her daydreams.

She imagined that her family was seated around the dining-room table waiting for the dessert to be brought in. Martha would make a grand entrance from the kitchen bearing a platter on which was a marvelous chocolate something-or-other, a delicacy as yet unnamed. The family would taste and then in one voice praise her wonderful cooking skill.

And since this was a dream, Arnold would say, "Martha, someday you will be a famous cook."

Martha sighed. Truth was so far from reality. As far as her family was concerned, she had no ability worth praising. Especially she had no cooking ability. Arnold would never let her forget the time she had tried to make a batch of fudge. It was supposed to be as rich and creamy and as good as his.

It would have been perfect fudge, too, if she had not got hold of the liniment instead of the vanilla.

Why Mamma kept the liniment in the kitchen cupboard Mamma herself couldn't explain. It was just that the bottle was handy so that she could rub Papa's back with big splashes of it when he strained himself haying or threshing. It had a strong, unmistakable odor. When Mamma was rubbing Pa's back in the kitchen, someone upstairs was sure to yell, "Put the cap back on the liniment!"

Therefore, it was an understandable mistake for Martha to grab the liniment instead of the vanilla. The bottles were the same shape and color; but the smell was different, Martha realized *after* she had added a generous amount to the cooling candy.

"Ask Martha for her recipe for liniment fudge," Arnold would tell his friends. "Good for backaches, sprains, or any muscular discomfort."

Well, all right. Let Arnold be the fudge maker of the

family. She could cook other things. She could fix eggs and fry potatoes and open cans of corn and beans. She could make a decent meal if she had to.

Martha had the responsibility for starting supper when her mother helped with the milking. She had got into the habit of burning the potatoes. She found it difficult to cook carrots, too, without burning them, and Arnold accused her of preferring the taste of "caramelized" carrots. The whole family tried to break her of this habit, for none of them happened to like her "burnt offerings." Mamma scolded. Janie held her nose. Arnold was especially fussy about it.

Martha defended herself: "A person can't just sit there and watch them boil, can she? A person might as well read a book and cook potatoes at the same time."

"But when a person gets so interested in reading that the person forgets about the potatoes, that person is a sad case," was Arnold's opinion.

Mamma agreed. "Martha should not read when she is trying to boil potatoes."

That conversation had taken place two weeks ago, and Martha could point to a perfect record of unburned potatoes since then.

She did wish that she could make something that would cause her family to sit up and take notice. How else could an eleven-year-old get attention? Janie could say cute things and everyone repeated them. When Martha tried to say cute things, they thought she was silly.

Martha remembered now that she had seen a picture of a beautiful chocolate cake in the *Farmer's Wife*. She would make it for dinner if her mother said she could.

She found her mother working in the newly planted garden. To Martha's question she answered, "Yes, you can try the cake. It's cool enough to do some baking today. Be sure to get a good cob fire going so that the oven is hot when you put the cake in."

In the summer the Martins did most of their cooking on a kerosene stove on the back porch. But since it had no oven, the cookstove in the kitchen had to be heated when they did any baking.

Martha called Janie to come watch her bake a beautiful cake. Janie was glad to leave the playhouse so that she could be a partner in such an adventure. She was even willing to run to the cobhouse for corncobs for the fire. Martha read through the recipe rapidly, and it did not take her long to stir up the batter and get the cake into the oven.

Then Martha surveyed the dirty dishes she had made. "Seems like I get cake batter all over myself and everything else when I bake," she sighed. "You didn't get it on the bottoms of your feets," Janie comforted her.

At dinner Mamma passed Arnold the plate with Martha's dessert. Arnold helped himself to a large square and took a big bite. He chewed hard for a few times and then held the piece up for closer inspection.

"What, may I ask, are these?"

Martha said quietly, "Cookies."

"Funniest cooky I ever ate," he replied. "Where did you get this recipe?"

Janie said, "Too bad it doesn't look like the picture, isn't it, Marty?"

Arnold stared at Martha.

Janie put her hand to her mouth in dismay. "Oh, I didn't mean to be a blabber mouse."

"All right," Martha said, "so it was supposed to be a cake and I forgot the baking powder. It just didn't rise."

Then Arnold laughed, and so did Mamma and Janie, and finally Martha. But even as she laughed, she knew that this would be another story to live down.

She could just hear Arnold saying: "Ask Martha for her recipe for *short* cake."

Martha decided then and there that she might as well quit trying to impress her family with her cooking ability. She would just cook ordinary things.

"And I'll just show that Arnold. I'll never burn the potatoes again, either," she vowed to herself.

The afternoon passed quickly, for Martha decided to reread *Anne of Green Gables*. She turned first to the part where Anne had dyed her red hair black and it had turned out green. Martha wished she had somebody she could read that part to. Mamma found her lying on her stomach on the window seat.

"I'm going out to chore now. Put on some potatoes for supper. Paul will be coming home early tonight."

Martha reluctantly left her book to set the table and put the potatoes on to boil. Then she went back to *Anne*. She was deep in the chapter where Gilbert had pulled Anne's red braid and called her "Carrots." Anne was so angry with him that she was just about to break her slate over Gilbert's head.

Just then Paul came in from threshing. He was in early so that he could get ready to go to town. Mary Miller did housework for a family in Lake City, and every Saturday night Paul went to get her and bring her home for Sunday.

Paul was in a zipping hurry. He zipped through shaving and he zipped upstairs and into his good clothes. Then he was through zipping and ready to snap. "Get me some milk from the milkhouse for my supper. Put out some bread and pie while I shine my shoes."

Martha could snap, too. "Stop ordering me around!"

But she got the milk pitcher and stamped out of the kitchen. When she returned, she plunked the pitcher down on the table so that some of the milk spilled over. Without a word she went back to the window seat and her book.

Paul has no reason to talk to me like that, she thought. Of course, he is in a hurry. She supposed Mary Miller did not enjoy waiting for him.

However, Paul did not usually snap at her. In fact, he usually took her part in arguments with Arnold. He had brought her a spoon from the World's Fair, and he often took her to church with him and Mary on Sunday nights. Martha began to feel guilty about her outburst.

Paul came into the dining room. He sat down beside her on the window seat.

"Thanks for the milk." Martha did not look up. He laid a nickel on her open book, then left. She heard him start his coupé and drive out of the yard.

The tears came to Martha's eyes. She was angry with herself, not with Paul. She had acted like a spoiled kid, and he had forgiven her. He wanted her to forgive him. This nickel was not meant for her college fund or for her mission bank, she knew. Paul had intended it for her private hoard, the money she was saving to spend in whatever way she liked. At the moment, she had no plans for spending it. Suddenly she knew what she was saving for: a wedding present for Paul and Mary, bought with her own money.

"Maybe if I told them I was going to buy them a wedding present, they would decide to get married." Martha giggled at her own joke.

A smell drifted in from the kitchen.

"Oh, no. Not again," Martha moaned. She made the kitchen in four long leaps and pulled the kettle to the back of the stove.

She had let the potatoes burn—again.

CHAPTER 7

Sunday, July 23
MARTHA MAKES RESOLUTIONS

THE BEST DAY of the week, of course, was Sunday. This Sunday promised to be especially good because the Martins had been invited out for dinner. Martha knew that the dinner would be something out of the ordinary, for Mrs. Kaufman always outdid herself for company. Should she skimp on breakfast so that she could eat more at dinner?

More important than the dinner invitation, however, was the possibility that Mary Miller might come to the Martin home for supper. Martha wondered if this might be an important day in *The Romance of Paul Martin*. There was a great similarity between Paul's romantic ups and downs and those of a radio serial. After the fifteen-minute radio story, the announcer would ask:

Will Shiela marry George?

Will the Plunketts lose their old homestead?

Will Dudley break his leg when he falls off the roof while shingling the barn?

Listen tomorrow for another chapter in this exciting story.

Paul's story was almost as exciting. Martha wanted to know the answers to some questions, too.

Would Mary Miller marry Paul Martin?

If so, when?

She knew that Paul had come home very late last night, and she would have liked to tease him about that; but teasing about a love affair was something that the Martins did not do, at least in front of their parents. Mr. Martin believed that love was a serious business, not to be taken lightly, not to be cheapened by teasing. Martha supposed he was right.

Some parents, however, were very jolly about love. It would have been fun to tell the family that she had written Paul's and Mary's names together, canceling out the like letters.

$$\text{P}\cancel{\text{a}}\text{u}\cancel{\text{l}}\ \cancel{\text{E}}\cancel{\text{l}}\text{d}\cancel{\text{e}}\cancel{\text{r}}\ \text{M}\cancel{\text{a}}\cancel{\text{r}}\cancel{\text{t}}\cancel{\text{i}}\text{n}$$
$$\cancel{\text{M}}\cancel{\text{a}}\cancel{\text{r}}\text{y}\ \text{C}\cancel{\text{a}}\cancel{\text{t}}\text{h}\cancel{\text{e}}\text{r}\cancel{\text{i}}\cancel{\text{n}}\cancel{\text{e}}\ \text{M i}\cancel{\text{l}}\cancel{\text{l}}\text{e r}$$

She had counted off the remaining letters saying, "Love, hate, friendship, courtship, marriage." She had ended with "hate," but she was sure that Mary must be misspelling her name. By taking the first *e* from *Catherine*, Martha counted off and came out with "courtship." She wished she could believe that marriage was in their future.

As she set the breakfast table, Martha thought hopefully that this could be the day for Paul and Mary to announce their engagement.

Sunday morning in the Martin home was like other mornings of the week in that the Martins slept no later than on weekdays. Cows do not know Sunday from Monday and are always ready to be milked early in the morning.

Breakfast was different, however. There were soft-boiled eggs and cold cereal instead of pancakes and oatmeal. Morning devotions consisted of reading the Sunday-school lesson. After the few chores and dishes were taken care of, everybody concentrated on getting ready for church.

Janie had a pink dress with a gathered skirt. The yoke was very short and the skirt began under her arms. Martha's Sunday dress was of red and white printed voile with a full skirt and a wide sash.

Paul and Arnold looked neat in white shirts, trousers, and shoes. Mamma knew why they looked so spotless. She had spent a half hour ironing each of the pairs of white slacks. She hated the ironing, but she said she wanted her boys to look decent.

Mamma herself was dressed in her best polka dot silk. She was less soft and huggable than on weekdays, but she looked very dignified.

"Come on, everybody. Henry Birkys have already driven by. It must be late." Papa was Sunday-school super-intendent, and he was always afraid that the clock was slow.

As they climbed into the car, Trixie jumped in too, making Papa more impatient with the delay of locking her in the barn.

Church was held in the Indian Grove School, just a mile and a half away. The Martins were Mennonites, and their group in this community was small. Most of the church members were related to each other. The minister was Mamma's cousin and so was Kate Birky. Since the Birkys had ten children, it was important for them to come to church just to make a crowd.

Delcie was wearing a pink lace dress today. It fit fine, but Martha could see where Kate had taken a deep hem. Evidently the Hanson daughter was tall and slender.

"Selma wanted this one, but you know Selma. She couldn't get the side buttons buttoned," Delcie said.

Martha wondered if Mamma would let her get pink lace next time she let her choose a dress from the catalog.

The girls found a desk together and waited for Mr. Martin to say, "Sunday school will open with the singing of the hymn on page 17." Page 17 was "Sunshine in the Soul," and it was a rousing song. Mr. Martin always started Sunday school with this one on a sunny morning. On cloudy or rainy Sundays he opened with "When the Mists Have Rolled Away," which was just as rousing but more suitable to the weather.

The congregation had just begun on the first song when

Martha noticed out of the corner of her eye that another family had come in. She had thought everybody was already here. Papa didn't usually start until he thought the crowd was complete.

Martha looked back to see who the late-comers were, then turned around quickly to exclaim to Delcie under the cover of the singing, "The Baronskis have come to church!"

Delcie had her mouth open for the word "soul" and it stayed open in surprise as she turned around to look at the notorious family that she had heard so much about.

Martha's Sunday-school class met in the cloakroom where they sat on the window sills. Martha said only a brief hello to Stefana as she joined the half-dozen children who were in the class. Martha had the opportunity to look at Stefana closely as the teacher, Delcie's oldest brother, started the lesson.

Stefana was wearing the black school dress. Her blond hair was combed back into tight braids as usual. And—would wonders never cease, Martha thought—she was barefooted!

Delcie and Martha looked at her feet and exchanged amused glances. Stefana must have noticed, for she tried to draw her feet under her skirt. Her fair skin colored to a pale pink.

After the classes were over, everyone met together again for church. Martha and Delcie sat together in one of the desks near the front of the room, leaving Stefana to go sit with her family. The minister started his hour-long sermon. Martha listened for a while, but nothing of what he said had any meaning for her. She looked at the picture card that she had received in Sunday school, and then there was nothing to do but sit.

For a while she sat and thought. She thought about that certificate of merit that was lying in Stefana's top dresser drawer. (Where else would anybody keep a certificate of merit?) How could a girl be so mean as to take a certificate she didn't really deserve?

"Let's play 'I know the song,' " Martha whispered to

Delcie. Delcie nodded. They began at the beginning of the hymnbook, and as one girl turned the page, each put one finger on the book if she knew the song. The one to touch the page first got a point. Since the girls knew the same songs, it was just a matter of deciding quickly by reading the title whether to pounce on the page or not. The game required no whispering, but sometimes the rustle of pages became noisy. When that happened, Martha's Aunt Fanny (who was Delcie's grandmother) reached out a long, black-sleeved arm and tapped Delcie on the shoulder.

Immediately after the benediction, Martha's mother came over to her. Martha was sure she was going to scold about playing the game, but Mrs. Martin leaned down to whisper in her ear, "Go over there and be nice to Stefana."

Martha grabbed Delcie's hand and together they approached the Baronskis. The father and mother, beaming and bowing, were trying to make conversation with their friendly neighbors. Stefana was standing back of her mother.

"Come on outside and we'll play 'Andy-over the woodshed,' " Martha suggested. The three girls went outside, but they agreed when they got to the woodshed that it was too hot to play. They sat down in the high grass under the big oak tree back of the schoolhouse.

Martha tried to think of something to say. She punched Delcie and Delcie said, "Did you notice my new shoes? They were in the box that the Hansons sent." Everybody looked at Delcie's shoes which were very nice and only a little too large. They were patent leather sandals, and Delcie's not-quite-clean toes were easy to see. Martha could tell that Delcie had done considerable racing around since she had taken her Saturday night bath.

At the mention of shoes, Stefana tried to hid her bare feet under her black skirt. Martha realized that Delcie had introduced the wrong subject for conversation.

In an effort to change the topic, Martha said quickly, "I just love your dress, Delcie. Don't you just love Delcie's dress, Stefana?"

Stefana spread her hands wide over her black skirt. "Yes, I think it is very pretty."

That subject wouldn't do, either. Martha searched her mind for something to talk about. The weather? They had covered that. The crops?

Just then a black car went by, and Martha said aloud the first thought that popped into her mind. "That looks like the sheriff's car. Did he find your place the other day when he was looking, Stefana?" Stefana's pink face grew rosy.

"This is the worst," Martha groaned to herself. "I should never have said that!"

"I have to go now. My folks are probably waiting for me." Stefana jumped up and ran off.

"That wasn't a very nice thing to say," Delcie's voice was accusing.

"I don't know why I did it. But that wasn't very nice of you to mention shoes, either."

Unhappy with themselves, with each other, and with Stefana, the girls decided that it was time to start urging their parents toward home.

When finally all of the congregation had left and Mr. Martin had locked the front door of the schoolhouse, Mamma exclaimed, "My, but I was surprised to see the Baronskis in church. I understood that they went to church in Gary."

Papa climbed into the car and they started home. "Probably decided it was too far to drive every Sunday. I hope they felt welcome here."

Martha didn't say anything. She knew that she had done her part to make Stefana feel very unwelcome.

"Now that threshing is over for us, I'll have to go down there for a neighborly visit," Mamma said.

The Martins stopped at home to feed the stock and to let Paul off to get his own car. Then they started for the Kaufman farm, where they were to have dinner.

Martha looked forward to a big meal. "I hope they have pie for dinner. I am so hungry now that I could eat six chocolate pies," she told her family.

"You would get sick. Anyway, I don't think your stomach would hold six pies," Janie protested.

"I was just aggravating," Martha said.

"Mamma, Martha is always aggravating. I wish she wouldn't."

Arnold said, "She means exaggerating, Janie. Exaggerate means to make something bigger than it really is. She could maybe eat two pieces of pie."

"Well," said Janie, "I wish she wouldn't exaggervate."

The Kaufman family consisted of seven boys and one daughter, Bonnie, ten years old. With six of the Martins and the John Good family who had also been invited, twenty-one people were anticipating Mrs. Kaufman's cooking.

Mrs. Kaufman had a strange habit of inviting people for dinner and then complaining: "I just should never have tried to have company this Sunday. We was so busy this week I didn't have no time to fix nothing. You'll just have to excuse the light table. I'm afraid these potatoes won't go 'round the second time, and this pie crust is tough as linoleum."

And Mamma would say, "Now, Lizzie, I know that you have never made a tough pie crust in your life, and that looks like enough potatoes for a family reunion."

"Come and get it, such as it is," Mrs. Kaufman called, inviting her company to the heavily laden table.

The men and boys ate at the first table and the women and girls at the second. Martha was numb with hunger by the time she sat down. But there was plenty of food left. Ham and chicken, white and sweet potatoes, noodles, corn, tomatoes, lettuce, coleslaw, pickles, beets, homemade bread, and applesauce. There were also canned peaches, white cake, and custard pie. Martha ate only a piece of pie for dessert. She felt that peaches were everyday food and white cake was a waste of good icing.

After dinner the boys all left for the pasture to play ball. The women washed the dishes, then sat down in the living room to talk. Martha and the girls found a corner of the back yard to spread their doll things out on the grass.

Soon the men came back from looking over the Kaufman livestock. They settled nearby on chairs brought from the kitchen by their host. The talk was of crops and farm business.

"Your boy about to get married, Elmer?" Mr. Kaufman asked Papa. Martha opened her ears.

"Not that I know of," Papa replied. "Do you know of a good farm for rent in case he does?"

"I've an idee that Warner's about to lose his farm. That might be for rent next year."

"Warner can't make his payments?" Papa asked. "Terrible the way farms are going nowadays. Do you figure this depression is about over?"

"Hard to tell," Mr. Kaufman answered. "How are things going with you?"

"Can't complain. Do you think I can get a crop of buckwheat yet before frost?"

John Good spoke up. "You know I just happened to hear over the radio that buckwheat is a good price this year. Farms over in Pennsylvania that raise buckwheat have some kind of blight this year."

Martha found her interest lagging in their conversation now; so she turned back to the problems of doll housekeeping.

At four o'clock all the guests got ready to leave, since they had cows to milk. When the Martins got home, they found that Mary and Paul had arrived just ahead of them. This was not Paul's Sunday to help with chores; but since he was at home, he put on his chore clothes and went out to the barn to help. Mamma, Mary, Martha, and Janie walked around looking at the garden and the chickens.

"Did you know that Harvey and Stella are engaged?" Mary asked Mamma. Harvey was Mary's brother.

"My, that's news! When did this happen?"

"He gave her the watch last night. She was wearing it today." It was the custom in her church for engaged girls to receive watches rather than rings.

"When will they be getting married?" Mamma asked.

"In September. Harvey is going to work for my father and they will live at home," Mary said.

They all wandered out to the barn. Martha knew that Paul would have been disappointed if Mary had not shown up to watch him milk.

Martha wished she knew whether Paul and Mary were planning to get married soon. Or were they planning to get married at all? They had been going together for five years, off and on. Everyone thought they were "going steady," but ever so often something would come up and Paul would not go to town on Wednesday and Saturday nights and Mary's father would have to make the trip to town to bring her home for the weekend. When Paul did not take Mary back to work on Sunday nights, did some other boy? Martha did not know.

Martha thought she knew why Paul wanted Mary Miller for a wife. In the first place, she was pretty. She wore her black hair in waves around her face and a bun in the back. She had very brown eyes and very white teeth. Besides being pretty, she was fun and she could cook. She was getting lots of practice in keeping house, working as she did for the Johnsons.

The women sat on the milk stools and watched the men finish the milking.

Janie was full of questions: "How old are you?"

Mary replied, "I am *very* old."

Janie persisted. "How old is *very* old?"

But Mamma said, "Hush, Janie. It is not polite to ask people how old they are."

Martha knew that asking ages was not polite, but she wished they could have found out. And when were they going to announce that they were engaged? Of course, a cow barn was not the proper place to announce an engagement. At supper, maybe?

After a supper of sandwiches, cake, and fruit salad, they sat around the table playing the game of remembering for Mary's benefit.

"Remember the time Arnold was memorizing 'Thanatopsis' and tried to plow right through the fence?" Paul said.

Everyone laughed, including Arnold.

Papa remembered, "And the time when Paul was in a hurry to go to town one Saturday night and he forgot to fill his car with gas? He had to walk all the way back home because all the neighbors had gone to town."

Then it was Paul's turn. "Remember when Pa took Janie to town with her dress on backwards? The front of her was all plain and the back was full of lace and fancy buttons."

Janie spoke up, "Remember the time when I was just a little kid I tried to go sledding in the summertime and bumped my nose and it bled?" Everybody laughed with Janie about the time when she was "just a little kid."

"Oh, look at the time! We will be late for church," Mamma exclaimed.

Martha realized that there would be no announcement about the engagement that night.

They all got ready to go to church again. Since their own group did not have evening meetings, the Martin family attended the church in town. Mary belonged to the town church, which was another branch of Mennonites. Paul and Mary asked Martha to ride with them in Paul's car.

The Martins had talked too long at the supper table. The congregation was already kneeling for prayer when they arrived. The men and women divided in the vestibule. Papa and the boys went to sit on the men's side of the church; Mamma, Mary, and the girls joined the women on the other side. They slipped into an empty space on a back bench, and Martha found herself beside Bonnie Kaufman. When the children were called to the front for the children's meeting, Martha went up with Bonnie.

The story lesson was presented by Mrs. Miller, Mary's mother.

"Can you imagine," Mrs. Miller asked, "being a stranger in your neighborhood? You don't know the people down the road. All your friends and relatives live far away; and when you go to school, all the children and the teacher are new to you. Then you would know how it feels to be a stranger."

"But," she continued, "if someone came to you and said, 'I want to be your friend. Let me play with you and help you make friends,' you would no longer be a stranger. This is what Jesus was talking about when He said, 'I was a stranger, and ye took me in.' When we are friendly to strangers, we are being a friend to God's Son."

"Is she talking to me? Is that part of the Bible, that we must be friendly to strangers?" Martha asked herself.

When church was over, Martha went home with her family and Paul took Mary back to her job at Lake City. Before she went to sleep that night, Martha thought over the day. It had been a good day, even though she had not found the answers to *The Romance of Paul Martin*. And then there was the terrible way she had acted with Stefana.

Martha was bothered by the story lesson that Mrs. Miller had told in church. She knew that it was her Christian duty to be nice to Stefana. But did the lesson apply when the girl was as stuck-up as Stefana? And when the girl's brothers probably were thieves? Surely under the circumstances, Martha was not expected to be a friend to Stefana. Maybe she could find some way to be nice to her without making her a friend. Oh, well. It was too mixed up in her mind to think about now.

What about tomorrow? "Tomorrow I will try to get along with Arnold," she resolved, but she knew that this resolution was almost too much for a mere eleven-year-old to carry out.

"How about piano practicing?" her conscience asked.

"I will practice if I remember, but I can't help it if I don't remember."

After all of these good resolutions toward perfection, Martha fell asleep saying her "Now I lay me."

CHAPTER 8

Friday, August 4
THE GHOST OF INDIAN GROVE

WHEN MARTHA awakened, she found that Janie was already up and gone. Martha decided to be lazy and enjoy the pleasure of having the whole bed to herself. Was the hush downstairs a before- or after-breakfast silence?

She settled herself comfortably to think. Her father and Paul had finished threshing yesterday just before a light rain had started in the late afternoon. The crew had finished the last rackful of bundles in the rain, and Paul and Papa had driven home, wet but happy to be through with threshing.

The end of the threshing season was always a time for celebration. There would be an ice-cream feed next week for all the families in the ring. John Good, the man who owned the rig, always provided the ice cream. This was something for Martha to look forward to.

What else could she look forward to during this long month before school started? Paul and Mary's engagement? Martha was getting discouraged with *The Romance of Paul Martin*. But how nice it would be if Mary and Paul would get married and live close by, maybe on the Warner place.

At that moment Martha had what she considered the inspiration that would solve all problems. Paul and Mary should rent the Craig farm where the Baronskis were now living! If the Baronskis would move, this would also solve the embarrassing problem of Stefana.

Martha had never carried out her good resolution to do something nice for Stefana. Her conscience had stopped pricking her because she had ignored it for so long. The trouble was that Martha had not been able to think of anything that she could do that would be "nice" enough, but not too "nice." She didn't want Stefana to think that she wanted to be her friend and she didn't want Stefana to think that—well, she didn't know what she wanted.

Martha was just about to consider getting up when her father's voice came up the stairway: "Martha! Get up. Come look at the buckwheat. It's blooming." Martha jumped out of bed and was dressed in a minute.

The whole family piled into the car to go look at the buckwheat. They found a pretty sight, a field of white blossoms set off by dark green leaves.

"How long will the blossoms last?" Mamma asked.

"The buckwheat will bloom for the rest of the summer. They tell me that there'll be some blossoms even at harvest-time." Papa had received his information from the county agent.

"Come on. Time to get back to work. Paul, as soon as you think it is dry enough, you can go help Baronskis with their haying. I promised him I would send a man."

Martha knew that when Papa needed an extra man for haying, he would call on the Baronskis. The neighbors always exchanged help for the big jobs, and she always wondered how they kept track of the work that they owed each other.

After a hasty breakfast, Martha started on the breakfast dishes. Mamma had a dishpan full of green beans that Henry Birky had brought over before Martha was up. Mamma sat on the other side of the table snipping beans while Martha washed dishes.

She rubbed the cream-colored chunk of homemade soap with her dishrag until she had a good suds in her pan. Then she poured the suds from one cup to another, admiring the rainbow colors of the bubbles. A few splashed on the floor.

"Stop suddling," Mamma said without losing her rhythm in bean snipping. The word *suddle* was not in the dictionary, but Martha knew what it meant. She stopped playing with the dishwater and started washing cups.

"Mamma, do you think Paul and Mary will ever get married?"

"Yes, I think maybe they will sometime. They have some problems to solve, though, before they can be married."

"Oh, my! What problems do they have?" Martha knew that Paul was short of money, but the buckwheat was growing nicely and looked like a good crop.

"They don't have a place to live, for one thing. They are welcome to live with us, but Mary wants her own place, and I can understand that. We lived with my folks for eleven months, and that was eleven months too long."

Martha did not hear her mother's last sentence. An entirely new train of thought entered her mind. "Say, wouldn't that be wonderful, Mary and Paul living right here with us!"

"And then the fact is, they just don't have much money. It takes quite a bit to start farming. Paul will have to use our machinery for a while before he can buy everything he needs. He should have a farm close to home."

Martha was no longer listening. Mary and Paul might live with them!

"Which room would they have?"

Her mother laughed. *"Man soll die Bärenhaut nicht verkaufen, ehe Man den Bären erlegt hat."*

"What does that mean, Mamma?" Martha asked.

" 'Don't sell the bearskin before you have caught the bear.' Or, in other words, 'Don't count your chickens before they're hatched.' "

Martha dismissed the proverb with a wave of the dish-cloth. "Oh, I just know they will get married."

"Mary and Paul are not even engaged yet. Maybe Mary will decide that she doesn't want to have all the problems of a farmer's wife." Mamma snipped beans quietly for a moment. "I hope she does marry Paul, though. I think she will make him a good wife."

Martha started her piano practicing right after she finished with the dishes, but she did not seem to accomplish much. She kept stopping to daydream. There was Mary Miller playing games with Janie and her, helping with dishes, making chocolate pie, and baking bread.

The daydream must have taken a noticeably long time, for Mamma called, "Martha, why aren't you practicing?" Martha quickly started on the scale of C.

She heard Papa come into the kitchen then. He said to Mamma, "I want to go to Lake City this morning for repairs for the milker. I'll be back by one."

Papa was shaving at the kitchen sink when Martha finished her practicing. She sat at the kitchen table to watch him. Mamma had gone out to the washhouse to put the beans on to boil.

"You all through with your chores?" he asked.

"I don't have another thing to do this morning."

Arnold came into the kitchen and sat down at the table with her. He, like Paul, had a problem, but it had nothing to do with getting married. It did have to do with money.

"I haven't banked a cent all summer. How can I ever go to college if I don't save money for it?" he asked.

Papa pulled the skin on his cheek tight and with his razor made a pink path through the white snowbanks of lather. "Arnold, you're so handy. Isn't there something you can make or grow that will sell?"

"I can make fudge, but I don't want to start a fudge business. And nobody needs my knot-tying ability," Arnold protested. Then he went into the living room.

"Want to go to town with me, Martha?"

"Oh, yes! But what about Janie?"

"Just you and me this time."

"Pa, come here. I want to show you something," Arnold called from the living room. They had their heads together over the volume of the encyclopedia when Martha went up-stairs to get ready.

Martha was ready by the time her father was. She had never felt so grown-up as she sat in the front seat of the car beside him. She was starched and unwrinkled, quiet and mannerly. A trip to town alone with Papa was a special occasion, and she had thought it worthy of her red and white gingham dress.

As they passed the Baronski farm, she said by way of making conversation, "Those Baronski boys! They are certainly wild-looking, aren't they?"

"Well, now, I don't know about that," her father answered mildly. "I think they are rather handsome boys. I'll admit they could do with a haircut a little oftener."

When they got to town, Mr. Martin parked in front of the dime store and said, "Meet me here in half an hour." Then he went about his business.

Martha decided to spend the time walking up and down the aisles of the dime store. As she entered the door, she was greeted by the delicious breeze from the noisy twirling fans; but she forgot about this luxury the minute she became aware of the mouth-watering aroma of the hot dogs in their little glass case. This was mixed with the smell of the relish pot and that of roasting peanuts. How could she wait to eat? She had never been so hungry.

Martha moved away from the lunch counter to look at the toiletries. These had a good smell, too. She loved the dime store. Martha walked along every aisle, buying nothing except in her imagination. If she had a dollar to spend, how would she spend it? Would she buy the imitation wrist watch with the hands that actually moved; or the set of doll clothes with real buttons and buttonholes? The wrist watch, she decided. She would really amaze the kids at Indian Grove with a watch like that, even though it didn't run.

She was waiting in front of the store for her father when he came.

"Let's eat lunch. What'll you have?"

Martha did not have to think before she exclaimed, "Hot dogs!"

They went into the dime store and perched on the high stools at the lunch counter. They each ate two hot dogs and a dish of chocolate ice cream. She was not nearly full when she had finished, but she didn't ask for more. She knew that when she grew up and had her own money and no one around to tell her not to, she would eat as many hot dogs as she wanted.

Together Martha and her father bought a sack of candy for Janie. Then they started home. As they drove out of town, they helped themselves to a little of the candy, knowing that Janie would not care. Before long, Mr. Martin noticed that half the candy was gone. Guilty but not really sorry, they closed the sack and tucked it out of temptation's way.

Then Martha exclaimed, "But this isn't the road home!"

Mr. Martin said, "We're going to stop at Glen Jackson's. Arnold found this article in the encyclopedia that says that honey made from buckwheat blossoms is something special, brings a good price. Might be Arnold could make a little money with bees. If bees make honey from buckwheat, maybe Arnold can make money from honey."

"Where will he get the bees?"

"Glen has quite a few hives, and I'm going to see if Arnold can borrow some. I don't know much about bees, but Glen does. We'll see what he has to say."

This is how it happened that when Martha and her father got home from town, they had two boxes of buzzing bees in the trunk of the car. Arnold was excited about his idea, and he and Janie joined Papa and Martha to drive out to the field to install the bees in their new quarters.

"Glen says that you can use his equipment to extract the honey. That is, if the bees take to the buckwheat," Mr. Martin said. "He says you can also get more hives if these work."

"Money from honey, money from honey," Janie sang as they drove back to the house.

Before he returned to the barn, Arnold said to Martha, "Next time you go to Indian Grove library, take back my knot book and bring me a book on beekeeping."

"All right. I might as well do that this afternoon."

She told her mother where she was going, picked up the key to the schoolhouse, and set off on her bicycle.

Martha arrived at Indian Grove and unlocked the front door with her key. The Martins kept a key to the schoolhouse because Mr. Martin held Sunday school there.

But there was something strange about the lock. After she turned the key, she discovered that the door was locked. Had it been unlocked? Had her father forgotten to lock it last Sunday? No, she remembered that the family had waited in the car while he locked up. Maybe Miss Williams had come in for a book and forgotten to lock the door after herself. That was not like Miss Williams, and hadn't she read in the paper that Miss Williams was in Colorado?

Inside the schoolhouse, Martha looked around with interest. Most things were just as they were on Sunday and on school days. The big stove sat cold and noiseless in the far corner. The blackboards were beautifully black, washed and dustless, inviting someone to take up the chalk and draw pictures. The wooden floors were shiny with oil, as they were only on the first day of school and after vacations.

There were some things that were different, too. The quietness, for example. No one raced through the swinging doors between the cloakroom and the schoolroom. No one chattered as they did at recess; there was no buzz of noisy children being quiet. Then, too, there was a different feel about the place. The coolness of the closed-up building hit her as she came in from the hot sunlight of the out-of-doors. It raised goose bumps on her bare arms.

Martha felt another difference in the schoolroom that she could not explain. She heard a thud that came from the closet off the cloakroom as though a book had fallen.

"Must be a rat in there." As Martha didn't like rats, she felt no urge to investigate.

Martha went over to the northeast corner where two doors covered the treasure that she had come to dig out. When she opened the doors, the educated mouse that lived there scampered away. Behind the doors were shelves of books, the best library of any country school in the county.

Martha looked at the Honeybunch books, but did not take them. Honeybunch was an old friend, but maybe she was a little young for a sixth grader. The Bobbsey twins were tempting, too, but Martha passed them by. She found what she had come for, the bee book. Then she chose a book about Indians and *Daddy Long-legs.*

As she was about to close the doors of the library, Martha heard a sound that was unmistakable. Somebody had sneezed! Again the noise came from the closet which was directly back of the library. Martha's goose bumps rose again. She stood perfectly still, but there was no further sound. Did a rat sneeze? Surely not like that. Someone was hiding in there who had a key or who had come into the building through an unlocked door. But why was the person hiding? Miss Williams wouldn't have hidden, nor would anyone who had a right to be there. A tramp? There had been one at the farm only yesterday. Or a criminal hiding out from the police in a deserted schoolhouse?

Martha wondered if she should leave through the door and lock it behind her. There was no other way out. She would have to go out into the cloakroom to get to the door, and the door of the closet was in the cloakroom. The nearest window was across the wide room, and she might have trouble getting a heavy window open.

"Well," Martha decided, "the person must want to stay hidden or he would have jumped on me before now. I will tiptoe out and shut the door without locking it."

She crept on her bare feet to the swinging door without making a sound. As she opened the door, it gave a loud squeal which frightened her as much as if a strange hand had tightened around her neck. Panicky with fright, she flew out the open front door and into the schoolyard. She dumped her armful of books into her bicycle basket and pedaled off furiously.

After she had gone about a quarter of a mile, she looked back. No one was following her. The schoolhouse door stood open as she had left it. She would have to ask Papa to come down to lock it tonight after supper. Miss Williams might not let her use the library again if she found the door open. She pedaled on home, wondering if she would ever again have the courage to go into the schoolhouse by herself.

Everything was quiet in the Martin house. Martha went directly to her room and made herself comfortable on her bed. She read for half an hour and then realized that she was hungry. This clearly was an emergency. She went to her dresser drawer and found the candy that she had squirreled away under the handkerchiefs. Martha arranged five caramels neatly on the quilt and ate one for every five pages that she read.

A pounding of feet sounded on the stairs. Janie danced into the room before Martha could slide the caramels under her book.

"Oh, Marty! Caramels! Kin I have one?"

"This is my share. You ate yours the day Papa brought 'em home."

Janie looked at the caramels; and as she looked, Martha could see that the candy became more and more mouth-watering.

"You," said Janie. "You are a selfish." She ran out of the room before Martha could see the tears in her eyes.

Martha had heard the tears in Janie's voice, however. But she peeled a caramel and turned back to her book.

"Janie loves candy as much as I do, maybe more," she thought.

"She feels terrible because you have some and she doesn't," her conscience said.

"Well, I saved mine. Why couldn't she save hers?" Martha reasoned.

"Because Janie is only five and hasn't learned how good

candy is when you save it," persisted the troublesome conscience.

Martha got up and went into her mother's room. From the window she could see her sister sitting in the swing by the back door, looking little and unhappy. Noiselessly Martha opened the screen wide. Taking careful aim, she tossed two caramels in Janie's direction. Miraculously, they plopped right into her little sister's lap. Janie laughed aloud, looking about for the source of this bounty, but Martha had disappeared from the window.

"My good deed for the day," Martha thought, pleased with herself. She went back to *Daddy Long-legs*.

When Mamma called her to help with supper, she closed her book reluctantly. "I wish I had someone to talk to about this. I wonder if other girls who read this guess how it will end."

At suppertime, Mamma was annoyed. "Where do all these flies come from, I wonder."

Martha thought of the open screen upstairs. "I guess I left a screen unhooked," she murmured and slipped upstairs to close it.

"Now why," she thought, "did I have to spoil my good deed by forgetting to close the screen?" Was it possible ever to live a perfect life?

Later at the supper table Mamma announced, "I walked down to visit with Mrs. Baronski this afternoon. I took her a dress pattern and showed her how to use it. She was very cheerful. Of course, they miss their friends in Gary and she was very glad for company. Their wheat and oats were good this year and they are getting a good herd started."

Mr. Martin was interested. "That so? I sure hope they make out. They are all hard workers."

Arnold and Martha exchanged glances.

Arnold said, "There was a police car at the Baronskis today. Do you suppose they are in some more trouble?"

Papa seemed unconcerned. "I don't think so. They seem to mind their own business pretty well."

Martha wondered how her father could be so easygoing. Why didn't he realize that probably the Baronski herd included Rosebud?

Paul said, "I thought we put up damp hay over there today. I told Mr. Baronski that I thought it needed more time to dry, but he didn't want to wait."

Papa spoke sharply, "Doesn't he know how dangerous it is to put damp hay in the mow? Did you tell him?"

"Yes, I told him. But you know how hard it is to make him understand. He didn't want us to waste our time; so we went ahead."

After supper Martha told her father about the sneeze in the schoolhouse.

"I doubt if you actually heard anything, but we'd better go down there and lock up," he said. "We don't want the school board to think we left the schoolhouse open."

When they drove into the schoolyard, they saw that the door was shut.

"I'll go see if it's locked," Mr. Martin said. He walked to the door and rattled the latch, but the door was locked.

"Can't figure it out," he said as he climbed back into the car. "Do you know anybody else who has a key?"

"Just Miss Williams."

"Must be the ghost of one of the Indians of Indian Grove," said Papa, and laughed at his own joke.

When they got back home, Janie was looking at the Indian book that Martha had brought from the library that afternoon.

"What is the woman doing in that picture?" she asked.

"Indian woman making dye," Martha read.

"Why is she making dye?"

"Oh, they dyed their clothes and their faces. Sometimes they even dyed their ponies."

"When their ponies got too old, did they died them?" Janie asked.

"Oh, it's your bedtime," Martha said, too tired to give Janie a lesson in homonyms.

90

CHAPTER 9

Sunday, August 6
THE DYED CALF

IT WAS Sunday afternoon. The Martins had not been invited out for dinner, and they had not invited company.

"It will be nice to stay home and rest," Mr. Martin said, and promptly after dinner he stretched himself on the davenport for a nap. The boys went up to their room for the same purpose.

After they had finished the dishes, Mamma said to Martha, "While I read to Janie, will you look through that new Sears catalog that came the other day and see if there are any nice dresses in my size? I'll need a new one for fall."

Martha made herself comfortable on the window seat and started looking at the catalog. She hunted first for a pink lace dress in her own size. There was not a single lace dress, pink or otherwise, in the girls' section.

Mamma joined her then, for Janie had fallen asleep.

"This would be pretty," Mamma said looking over those in her size. "I always like dark blue with white polka dots."

"But your summer dress is white with dark blue polka dots."

Mamma sighed. "I wish I could wear those dresses with big roses. It is such a trial to be heavy."

A voice from the davenport in the other room said,

"Why don't you just resign yourself to your fate and forget about your size? You are a stout woman."

Mamma bristled. "The catalog says I am a stylish stout," she replied.

The only answer to that was a snore from the other room.

"Well, I think I will take a nap, too," Mamma said. "It is such a drowsy day." She went upstairs to her bedroom.

"How dreary!" Martha thought. "Nothing to do, nobody to play with."

She went out to sit in the swing by the back door. Since she had nothing else to do, she decided to do a little daydreaming. What should she be this time? A schoolteacher? A lady preacher? An authoress! She would write a book. Everybody in the world would read her book and she, Martha Martin, would bring fame and glory to the family name. Her book would be about the life of an elegant young woman named Annabelle Worthington. The first chapter would begin thus: "Annabelle Worthington, dressed in elegant green satin, came into the room."

Came was too ordinary a verb. *Glide* would be better. What was the past tense of *glide?* Probably the same as *ride, rode, ridden.* Or was it of the same family as *slide, slid, slid?* "Annabelle Worthington glode into the room."

Arnold and Paul came out the back door and started for Paul's coupé.

Martha said, "How is this for the first line of a book: 'Annabelle Worthington, dressed in elegant green satin, glode into the room'?"

Her brothers stopped and Arnold asked, "What do you mean, glode?"

"You know, *glide, glode, glidden.*"

Arnold shouted with laughter. "You'd better learn some more grammar before you try to write a book."

Paul said, "Otherwise it is a good beginning. I can't wait to hear more about the elegant Annabelle. Come on, Arnold. Let's get over to Millers."

Martha suggested: "I could go with you. I haven't anything else to do."

"No," Paul said, not unkindly. "There won't be any other kids there."

They hurried off, and soon the blue coupé was scooting down the road.

Martha closed her eyes and went back to her daydream, this time in the person of the beautiful Annabelle. The green satin looked gorgeous with her blond curls as she glid (what *was* the past tense of *glide?*) into the room.

Someone said, "Hello, cat eyes."

Martha's greenish-brown eyes flew open. Howie Birky was standing over her.

"Where did you come from?"

"Your folks home?"

"Yes, but Arnie and Paul aren't home." If Howie was here by himself, she wanted him to know that there was no one here for him to visit. But Howie yelled to the car parked behind the shed, "Come on in," and left her.

Louie and Kate Birky and Delcie came up the walk. They explained that the boys were going to a ball game and had just dropped them off. The parents went on into the house to wake up the Martins, and Delcie joined Martha on the swing. She had on her familiar patched overalls.

"What shall we do?" Martha asked. "And we had better get started before Janie wakes up."

"Let's go fishing down by the bridge."

"Oh, let's. Arnold never lets me go with him. He says I talk too much. But I don't."

"Well, come on then. Let's get going."

They told Mrs. Martin where they were going, then got fishing poles from the shed and started down the road. The sun was hot and the sand was warm to their bare feet.

They were glad to reach the bridge and scramble down the steep bank to reach the cool shade underneath. There was an eddy of sand where another ditch joined this one. They stuck the poles in the sand and then sat down to talk.

Martha splashed into the shallow water along the sand eddy. "I'm Marco Polo, and I'm discovering the Grand Canyon. This is the Colorado River."

Delcie protested. "I wasn't very good at geography, but I don't think Marco Polo discovered the Grand Canyon."

Martha only laughed. "I know he didn't, but he's the only explorer I can think of right now. Use a little imagination. This little bay here in the sand is Hudson's Bay, and this little mountain here is Pikes Peak."

Delcie knew enough geography to play a mixed-up game like that; so before long they had the area under the bridge laid out in a crazy map of the United States. They were so absorbed in their play that the thunder of a car crossing the planks of the bridge over their heads frightened them. The car turned east and drove away from them, and they saw that the Baronskis were driving somewhere.

Martha had an inspiration. "Since the Baronskis are not at home, let's go look at their cows and see if they have Rosebud in their herd."

Delcie was uncertain. "What if they didn't all leave? One of them may have stayed home. We couldn't see how many were in the car."

"Oh, come on. Of course they all left. They probably are going to Gary to see their relation." She didn't say that Gary was in the other direction.

"Well, all right."

They climbed back to the road and slipped under the barbed-wire gate into the Baronski pasture. The cows were grazing up near the farm buildings. Delcie and Martha approached the herd without fear, for they knew that milk cows were gentle and harmless. The cows merely lifted their heads and stared at them.

Martha knew what kind of calf to look for, but Delcie had never seen Rosebud. "She will be half grown, light brown, with a star on her forehead. See that one?" Martha pointed to a young heifer. "About that big, but lighter colored. In fact, that one looks quite a bit like Rosebud."

94

"Maybe the Baronskis dyed her."

"What do you mean, 'dyed her'?" Martha asked.

"You know, the way the Indians dyed their skin with bark and things. Our history book says they dyed yarn for weaving—"

"We aren't talking about Indians. We are talking about Poles and a calf."

"Well, maybe they put something on Rosebud to make her darker so that no one would know her."

Martha remembered hearing that sometimes stolen ponies were dyed so that they would not be found out. "I'll bet that's what happened. I just know the Baronskis took her."

They were startled by a shout coming from the farmyard. They turned to see Thaddeus Baronski by the fence, yelling something at them in Polish. Then slowly and distinctly he shouted, "Do not scare the cows."

Delcie and Martha turned and started to run back to the bridge. After a few minutes, they glanced behind them. They were not being chased; so they slowed down to a walk. Thaddeus was still leaning against the fence.

Delcie scolded, "Next time you're so sure nobody is home, go knock at the door and find out."

"Anyway, we found out what we wanted to know. Let's quit fishing. I'd like to go look at that hide-out again."

They pulled up their fishless poles and set off through Paul's cornfield in the direction of the hide-out. They walked along the pasture fence, but between the rows of corn. Because they could not see much but corn, they were surprised by a flap of wings, then the deliberate ascent of two large hawks.

"What are those buzzards doing around here?" Delcie asked.

"Never mind that. Come on. We are just about there."

They passed the pasture and walked along the edge of what had been the oats field. Arnold had been plowing there yesterday. Half the field was turned over into black furrows.

They now walked along the bank of the small ditch where the willows grew thick.

Delcie followed Martha through the tunnel-like path that led into the little clearing. They stood up tall but they could not see over the green willows. They sat down in the cool shade.

Delcie looked around with new appreciation. "I would like a place like this for myself. Nobody could find me here unless they knew how to look."

"You know, this is probably where the Baronskis dyed the calf. They could have used ditch water. Or don't you need water for that kind of dye?"

"I suppose you make it with water, just like you make dye for a dress," Delcie said.

Martha said, "It's a funny thing. I told Arnold about the hide-out, thinking he would get all excited about it. But he didn't say much."

Delcie picked up something from the grass. "Look, here is a bread crust. Otherwise the place is as clean as a whistle."

Martha examined the crust. "That was left here not too long ago. It looks like the Baronskis still use this place. Say, do you think that older boy would follow us here?"

They listened for a moment, but they heard only the sound of the wind rustling the willows.

Martha said, "We wouldn't be able to hear anyone coming. Let's go."

They left the willow hide-out and started home through the plowed field. It would have been easier and shorter to cut across the pasture, but they were barefooted and the pasture was full of thistles.

"Those hawks are still over there in the pasture," Delcie observed. "Wonder what they want over there."

When they got back to the house, they found that Paul and Arnold had come home to help with the milking.

"Come on, you two. Help me round up the cows," Arnold called as he went into the house to change his clothes.

Martha got her shoes. Then she and Arnold mounted Lady. Delcie, who could ride anything, jumped on Bessie.

As the cowboys rode near the herd, Arnold pulled Lady up short and said to Martha in a low voice, "Who's that walking among the cows?"

Martha followed his glance and saw someone in the middle of the herd. Arnold urged Lady on, and in a moment they were behind the man.

Arnold jumped on his back in a flying leap from the saddle. They began a struggle that Arnold, with his slight build, might not have started had he thought it over.

Martha saw that help was needed, and so she slid off Lady's tail. She grabbed at a flying arm which hit out at her and tumbled her to the ground. Martha sat down hard, but she got up fast, for she had fallen into one of the many bull thistles that dotted the pasture.

Delcie slid off Bessie and came running to join them, yelling at the top of her voice. With the help of the girls, Arnold managed to tie the man's hands behind his back with a rope from his pocket. As he finished a neat square knot, Arnold said with satisfaction, "I told you my knot-tying ability would come in handy sometime."

Then he recognized his victim. "Casimir Baronski!" He didn't know whether to be angry or embarrassed. "What are you doing in our pasture?"

Casimir spoke in a torrent of excited Polish.

"Can't you speak any English?" Delcie demanded.

"I'll untie you, Casimir. I'm sorry I jumped on you. Come talk to my father."

Arnold walked with Casimir, leaving the girls to follow on Lady and Bessie. On the safety of Bessie's broad back, Delcie began pulling thistles from her feet.

"That was a good piece of yelling you did there," Martha commented. "I think you scared Casimir to little bits."

"I wasn't yelling at Casimir. Just at these thistles."

Arnold came up beside her. "That sure was a pretty

97

sight, the way you glode off that thistle after you landed on it, Fastest glodding I've ever seen."

Martha shrugged. "Just wait. Someday I'll be a famous authoress, and you'll come begging me to remember that you are my brother."

"I'll hold my breath until that day," Arnold replied.

When they got to the barn, Mr. Martin listened to Casimir carefully. Then he spoke. "As near as I can make out, they ran out of gas over on the river road. He was walking across the fields to get home by the shortest way. Did you run out of gas, Casimir?"

Casimir nodded, happy to be understood.

"Well, then, let's get some gas and get to the car. We'll take care of you."

After Mr. Martin and Casimir had gone, Martha and Delcie talked over the incident.

"I still think he was looking for another calf," Martha insisted.

"No, I don't think so," Delcie said. "When you try to talk to him, he seems like a nice enough guy. I believe him —he ran out of gas. If anybody took Rosebud, it was that Thaddeus."

"Yes, I guess it was Thaddeus."

"Stefana wasn't in church today with her folks. Do you think she is sick?"

"No, she probably didn't want to come," Martha said uncomfortably.

The Birky boys returned then and Delcie had to go home. "See you next Sunday," they said to each other.

Later that evening, as they were driving home from church, Martha gave more thought to what she wanted to be when she grew up. She wondered if she wouldn't really rather be a schoolteacher than an authoress. Whatever she decided to become, the sad fact was that it would be years before she could achieve fame and fortune.

What could she do here, now, in August, 1933, that would bring her just a small taste of glory?

CHAPTER 10

Tuesday, August 8
ARNOLD SETS AN EXAMPLE

WHEN MARTHA had finished the dishes, she went to join her mother in the swing by the back door. Mrs. Martin was busy cutting sweet corn for canning. Martha watched as she drew the butcher knife through the corn, then pressed the knife quickly down over the length of the cob to get all the milk from it.

"Mamma, what can I *do?*" Martha wailed. "There is nothing to *do*. Couldn't I go someplace and *do* something?"

"I'm afraid I can't think of a place for you to go."

"Don't you want me to be happy?" Martha asked.

"Yes, but I don't think that happiness is the most important aim in life."

"Now, Mamma, Thomas Jefferson put it in the Constitution that we have the right to life, liberty, and the pursuit of happiness. I would like to pursue a little happiness."

"That reminds me of a quotation we wrote in our copy books when I was a girl. We had to memorize all those quotations, whether we understood them or not.

Happiness in this world, when it comes, comes incidentally. Make it the object of pursuit and it is never attained.

Nathaniel Hawthorne said that."

"I don't know if I quite understand it," Martha said.

Mamma thought for a minute. "We had another one:

Happiness is a butterfly, which, when pursued, is always just beyond your grasp, but which, if you will sit down quietly, may alight upon you.

I don't know who said that."

Martha considered this one. "Well, I guess it means that you shouldn't run after happiness. Anyway, I do need something to do."

"Go get a library book," her mother suggested.

Martha went into the house to look over her books.

Although Martha had been to the Indian Grove library only four days ago, she found that she was again out of reading material. Finding a book that she hadn't read was getting to be a problem. Maybe she should try Arnold's books, *Ivanhoe* or *Silas Marner*. Or she could get the Blue Bonnet series and read through those again.

The question was, Did she have enough nerve to go back and risk meeting up with that ghost?

She decided to ride over and look at the front door of the schoolhouse. If she saw the imprint of a ghostly hand on it, she would turn tail and come home as fast as she could pedal. She took the key from the hook in the kitchen, piled her books in the bicycle basket, and set off.

The schoolhouse door *looked* locked. When Martha jiggled the latch, she found that it was. She opened the door with her key, but before she entered the building, she stood in the open doorway peering into the gloomy cloakroom; she listened with both ears for any ghostly sneeze, swish, or rustle. There was not a sound.

Martha went to the library and opened the doors. She jumped when the little mouse who lived there scampered away. Then she laughed at herself. There was nothing to fear at Indian Grove today. After all, the door had been locked.

She set about choosing her books, picking out one and then another, reading a little here and there. Then she turned to the space where the Blue Bonnet series was shelved. But today there was a twelve-inch gap in the row of books. All of the Blue Bonnet books were gone.

Who besides Martha could be using this library? Miss Williams had told her last summer when she gave her permission to use the library that she was the only one who had this special privilege.

"None of the other children are so crazy about books as you are, and I know I can depend on you to take care of them," Miss Williams had said last year.

Would Miss Williams have taken the Blue Bonnet books herself? No. She was not interested in that kind of book. Martha did not believe in ghosts. But she wished she had an explanation for the queer things that were going on. A ghost who read girls' stories was unsettling.

Hastily she took an armload of Ruth Fielding books and left the building. She had read these before, but she didn't want to spend any more time looking for others.

She was almost home when she had to pull her bicycle off to the side of the road to let the mail lady pass. She stopped at the mailbox, then, and found a letter addressed to herself.

"Such familiar handwriting. From Boulder, Colorado. It isn't Aunt Louise's." Straddling her bike there by the mailbox, she ripped open the envelop and found a letter from Miss Williams:

Dear Martha,

I am having a wonderful time vacationing in Colorado. It is so cool that we sleep under blankets every night.

Martha stopped to consider this as she wiped her moist face with her skirt.

I suppose you have been busy helping your parents on the farm. I hope you and Stefana have become good friends. Probably by this time you have found out how much she loves to read, almost as much as you do.

I had meant to write to all my students, but I find I don't have the time. I know that I can depend on you to give my best wishes to Stefana. I am looking forward to seeing both of you in school in a few weeks.

Sincerely yours,
Berniece Williams

Martha put the letter back in the envelope and picked up the rest of the mail. What should she do about that letter? She wanted her mother to know about it, but she didn't want her mother to say, "Now you go right over there and visit Stefana and let her read the letter." Stefana probably wouldn't even let her in the house.

At the supper table that night Paul asked Arnold, "Did you look at your bees today?"

"Yes. They seem to feel right at home there in the buckwheat field."

"Maybe you can make so much money with bees that you won't miss the calf money," Mamma said hopefully.

Arnold shook his head. "These bees will have to produce a couple of barrels of honey to make as much money for me as Rosebud would have made. It makes me mad every time I think of it. Pa, why don't you go ask Mr. Baronski where they got that Brown Swiss calf that runs with their herd? Just asking wouldn't hurt anything. I'm sure it is Rosebud."

"It is none of our business where they get their cows," said Mr. Martin.

Arnold persisted, "Maybe we should go down there some night and put a rope around her neck and lead her home."

Mr. Martin laid down his fork, looked straight at Arnold, and spoke louder than usual. "No. I won't have any such talk. Even if that calf is Rosebud, we will not steal her back. You don't right a wrong with a wrong."

"Well, isn't there anything we can do about it?"

"Our only duty is to set an example of neighborliness for the Baronskis, no matter what they do." That closed the subject as far as Papa was concerned.

Martha went to bed that night to dream of brown calves and buzzing bees and a ghost going "WOO-oo." The calves bawled. The bees buzzed. The ghostly shriek rose and fell.

Martha awoke to discover that the noise in her dream was actually the distant sound of the siren coming through the open window from Cummings, five miles away. Always before she had recognized the sound as the noon whistle, but here in the middle of the night the siren could mean only one thing: fire.

Fully awake now, she ran to the north window to see if she could see anything. She could see nothing; so she unhooked the screen and crawled out on the porch roof so that she could look east and west. In the west the sky was a pale gray-yellow, as if the sun were coming up in a haze from the wrong horizon.

She ran to her parents' room and knocked on the door. "Papa, there's a fire. Don't you hear the siren?"

The bed springs creaked as her father sat up quickly. "Is it on our place?" he asked, wide awake.

"No, it's west of here. I can't tell whose place it is."

The boys were awake now, and they tumbled over each other coming out of the doorway of their room, fastening the buckles on their overalls. They all started down the stairs in a rush, Mamma and Janie tagging along in their nightgowns. The family, all of them barefooted, trooped outside. Arnold raced out to the road where he could get an unobstructed view.

"It's the Baronski farm," he shouted back. "It's their barn."

"That damp timothy hay," Papa exclaimed. "Come on, boys, let's get down there to see if we can help."

"I will come too," Martha said, but Papa wouldn't have it.

"You stay home out of the way."

In a moment they were roaring down the road in the Martin car.

Mamma, Janie, and Martha watched from the road as the building blazed. They were too far away to see all the details, but even from half a mile they could see the outlines of cars as they arrived at the fire. The farm buildings were located on a small hill, and the blaze made the picture brighter than day. Neighbors kept arriving from all directions. Several times the Martins stepped out of the road to let a speeding car go by.

Apparently there was nothing the men could do to save the barn. The flames leaped high and the smoke rose in a straight black column. All at once the structure fell to the ground, leaving only a glowing mound of embers.

"That was quick," Mamma said as they went back to the house. "They had all their wheat stored in that barn, besides the hay. Those poor people."

The men soon came home to give their report.

"We couldn't do a thing but watch it go," Papa said. "Lucky the house is so far from the barn and there was no wind. Remember ten years ago when Johnson's hay burned and their two other barns caught fire, too?"

Martha asked, "What started the fire?"

Arnold answered, "Spontaneous combustion."

"What's that?"

Arnold was glad to explain. "When damp hay is put in the mow, it sometimes starts heating and gets so hot that it sets fire to itself. The side of the barn where the hay was stored went up like paper. The wheat burned slower."

Mamma said, "What I want to know is how the telephone operator found out about it so that she could blow the siren. Baronskis don't have a phone."

"Oh, John Good happened to see it and called in," Papa said. "The Baronskis didn't even know their barn was on fire until the first car got there. And the fire department from Cummings got there in time to watch it cave in."

Paul said, "I tried to talk to Thaddeus a little. I gathered that he and Casimir would probably go back to Gary to see if they can get on at the mills again. They'll need cash to buy winter feed for their herd."

Papa nodded. "Craig can build a new barn now. He can afford it." He looked at the clock. "Three o'clock! Everybody back to bed. Five o'clock will come before we are ready for it."

They all went to bed again, Mamma fretting at them for having dirty feet and nobody wanting to take time to wash them. Martha knew that she was too excited to sleep. She thought about Stefana and wished she were on good terms with her so that they could go poke around the burned buildings. This was a great misfortune for the Baronskis, but of course it didn't change the fact that the brothers were thieves. Maybe all of them would go back to Gary now. That would solve Martha's problem of how to be nice to Stefana without making her a friend.

Just then Janie stepped on Martha's stomach as she scrambled out of bed. "Excuse me, Martha," she replied to Martha's groan. "Did I make a dent in your stomach? I want to get up and go look at the Baronskis' splendid combination."

It was not until Janie was at the foot of the stairs that Martha realized that the morning had arrived without her having gone to sleep. Or had she? With a little more thought, she figured out that by "splendid combination" Janie meant spontaneous combustion. Would that child never learn to speak correctly? She was so exaggerating.

Just after breakfast Mr. Baronski arrived at the back door to ask Papa if Arnold and Paul could plow for him. Thaddeus and Casimir had gone to see about jobs in the steel mills. They would work there until spring, or at least until they were laid off. The Baronskis needed the cash money for feed for the herd.

Mr. Baronski said he would pay the Martin boys two dollars a day for plowing. Martha thought that this was a good opportunity for Paul to add a little to his getting-married fund. Arnold, of course, would add his earnings to his college fund.

Papa had lots of farm work of his own to do. He had planned to have the boys plow for him. But he wanted to help Mr. Baronski since he had had such a heavy loss from the fire. He decided that he could spare the boys. They were to plow from Wednesday through Saturday, using both the tractor and the horses.

That afternoon when Mamma sat down to rest, Martha showed her the letter from Miss Williams.

"My, that's a nice letter. Why don't you go down to Stefana's this afternoon and show it to her?"

"Oh, Mamma, it's too hot. I will tomorrow. But Stefana hasn't been very nice to me, and I'm not sure she will appreciate a visit."

Mamma looked at her sharply. "I can't imagine Stefana not being nice."

Martha went outside. It was hot. "Janie, let's go swimming in the horse tank."

The girls pumped clean water into the tank that the family used in summer for a bathtub. It was almost as good as swimming in the Kankakee River back of Birkys' farm.

Martha was alone in the tank when Paul and Arnold came in from the Baronski fields to clean up. They sat down on the grass to take off their muck-filled shoes. Martha was lying out of sight in the tank. She supposed she should have made her presence known, but her brothers started such an interesting conversation that she did not want to miss it.

Paul said, "Mr. Baronski told us he would pay us, you know. It's up to you if you think we should take the money. For my part, I would be willing to do his plowing just to be neighborly."

Arnold did not speak for a moment. Then he said, "It is hard to feel neighborly when I know his boys stole my calf."

Paul was silent, and Arnold continued, "But I guess I have been around Pa too long. I don't think it is right to take his money when he had such a big loss from the fire, even if his boys are thieves. Pa is right; I realize that. All we can do is show the Baronskis how to be neighborly."

Paul and Arnold shook the dirt out of their shoes and socks and went into the house. They had given Martha something to think about. Each of them was giving up good money. Let's see—four days times two dollars—eight dollars that they could have used themselves. Arnold was making the greatest effort because he felt so bitter about his calf.

If Arnold could do something noble like that, couldn't she show Stefana that she, Martha Martin, could be neighborly, too, even if Stefana had stolen the certificate of merit away from her?

Martha climbed dripping from the tank. As she got into her dry clothes, she made a resolution: Tomorrow—no more putting off—tomorrow she would go to see Stefana.

CHAPTER 11

Tuesday, August 15
TRIXIE MAKES A DISCOVERY

THE *Dance of the Rosebuds* sounded more like a stumble as Martha plunked her way through it.

"Pretend that each note is a pretty rosebud," the teacher had said.

"Each note is an ugly, sticky, impossible, pointed, thorny thorn," Martha said and crashed all the pretty roses together into an unpleasant discord.

Paul put down his account book. A light shower had driven the men inside, and he was trying to figure his income and expenses. He came over to sit on the piano bench with Martha.

"Are you having trouble?" he asked.

Martha nodded. A tear rolled down to the tip of her chin. "I hate and despise piano lessons. I wish Papa and Mamma would let me quit."

"They let me quit and I wish they hadn't. If I had kept on, I could be playing Chopin. All I can remember is this." He plunked out a simple little march slowly, and with a number of wrong notes. Martha recognized it as *March of the Little Sages* and laughed in spite of herself.

Paul continued, "Piano lessons are important. If you stick with them, maybe I can make them worth your while."

Paul went back to his account book and Martha started practicing again. After a few minutes, Paul put away his book and got out the Sears catalog. Janie came into the living room and the two of them looked through the catalog quietly so as not to disturb Martha. Naturally Martha was curious to know what they were whispering about. As she finished practicing, Paul sealed his letter addressed to Sears, Roebuck and Co., Chicago, Illinois.

"What are you ordering?" Martha asked.

"I sent for a pair of overalls," he answered. Janie giggled, and Paul frowned at her.

"Where did you go last night after supper?" Martha asked.

"Well, aren't you full of questions? I went to Millers."

Martha's eyes opened wide. "On a Monday night when Mary isn't home! What for?"

"Mary is taking her week's vacation and she *is* at home. What else would you like to know, Question Mark?"

Martha laughed. "Nothing. Now I know all there is to know," and she took the letter to the mailbox for him.

This happened on Tuesday morning. The rain stopped before noon; so Martha decided that this was the time to carry out the resolution she had made a week ago. Every day since last Tuesday she had told herself that she should go over there and every day she had found a good reason for not going. But Martha knew that it was her duty to be nice to Stefana and she was determined to be neighborly.

That afternoon she asked Janie to go down to the Baronskis with her. Maybe with Janie along, the meeting would go more pleasantly.

The girls went to the back door of Baronskis' house. Mrs. Baronski had just finished baking, and a smell of home-made bread came drifting through the screen door. Martha realized how hungry she was for warm homemade bread. Next to pie and cake, she liked fresh bread and jelly. Mamma did not do much baking during the hot summer.

Mrs. Baronski came to the door in answer to their knock.

She was a large woman, much the same shape as Mamma, but shorter. She had lots of pleasant wrinkles around her eyes and mouth.

"Hello, girls, come in, come in. How are you, and how are your mamma and papa?" Mrs. Baronski asked in her broad Polish accent.

"We are all fine. Is Stefana home?"

"Isn't that too bad, now, she isn't. She is visiting her auntie in Gary. It was kind of lonesome here on the farm this summer, and she is used to the city. So we let her stay in Gary."

Martha felt a twinge of shame. If she had been friendlier, Stefana would not have been so lonesome on the farm. Oh, well. Stefana probably didn't want her company anyway.

"You girls come in. Sit in the kitchen while I bake," Mrs. Baronski invited.

They took chairs at the kitchen table. Newly baked loaves of rye bread were lying on the table on a white towel. Their fragrance was tantalizing. Martha had never been so hungry in her life. Janie left her chair to whisper in Martha's ear. Martha shook her head and replied, "Not now. When we get home."

Mrs. Baronski smiled and said, "You are hungry. Have some Polish rye bread." She spread each of them a piece of fresh, warm bread with butter and jelly.

Mrs. Baronski was a very understanding person, Martha decided. She had understood Janie's whispering.

The girls visited with Mrs. Baronski. Janie did most of the talking, and Mrs. Baronski nodded as if she understood everything that Janie said. Martha was glad she had brought Janie along.

When the girls made their good-bys, Mrs. Baronski told them to come back when Stefana came home. Martha walked home with her do-good intentions deflated. She had gone with the idea of showing the Baronskis how neighborly she could be. Now she had the feeling that Mrs. Baronski was the neighborly one.

When she got back to the Martin farm, Mamma told her that Papa needed her help. She found him in the driveway of the corncrib, sharpening the mower sickle. Mr. Martin looked as though he were riding a bicycle as he moved his feet up and down on the pedals of the grindstone, but he didn't get anywhere. Martha helped him by holding up the end of the long blade while he sharpened each little triangle in the sickle.

"I'm late getting that pasture mowed," he scolded himself. "Those bull thistles and wild lettuce will take over the grass if they are left to go to seed."

Martha watched the sparks fly from the grindstone as he held the blade against it. "Papa, I've been thinking. If those Baronski boys actually did steal Arnold's calf, do you suppose their folks and Stefana know they did it?"

"In the first place, we should not say that the Baronski boys stole the calf because we have no proof of it. And if they did, I'm sure their parents don't know about it. Mr. Baronski has been a good neighbor and not the kind of man who would take anything that does not belong to him."

"But even if Stefana is a nice girl, I'm not sure I want to be friends with a girl whose brothers *might* be thieves," Martha insisted.

"Even if Stefana's brothers are thieves, she needs good people for friends."

Martha was almost convinced. "Maybe I should ask Stefana down here to play with me as soon as she comes home from Gary."

"You do that. Now let's see if this will cut those weeds."

Mr. Martin put the blade on the mower; then he hitched up the team. As he was ready to start for the pasture, Trixie appeared and jumped up on the tongue of the mower.

Papa said, "O.K. You can ride to the pasture. But when I put the sickle down and start mowing, off you go. Your grandfather lost a leg by getting in the way of a mower."

Now that she had helped Papa, Martha was free to play. There would not be many more days left for playing.

This was the middle of August and school would be starting soon. Then playing would have to wait for recesses, noons, and after school.

Martha joined Janie in the playhouse. They had arranged this playhouse in an empty corner of the corncrib. The sides of the crib were made of boards nailed an inch or so apart; so you could see out but still feel in. The girls put boards across the corner between the slats and had convenient shelves.

Together they gathered dry, brown dock seed. The seeds looked something like freshly ground coffee. Martha looked forward to the time when the milkweed pods would be ready to open. The seeds were arranged in the shape of lovely little fish with delicate fishy scales.

"Now let's play house," Martha said. "I will be a grownup lady and my name is Annabelle. I think Annabelle is the prettiest name there is."

"My name is May," Janie said. "May is the prettiest name."

"Let's wear our high heels." They had made the highheeled shoes by nailing spools to pieces of wood. The girls fastened them to their bare feet with rubber bands.

"My dress is red satin," Janie said, spreading her soiled cotton skirt over the nail keg she was sitting on.

"How do you do, May? What a lovely red satin dress you are wearing," Martha said in her most beautiful voice.

"You look george-ous yourself in that purple velvet, Annabelle," Janie returned the compliment.

A high-pitched voice came from somewhere. "Howdy do, Annabelle. Howdy do, May. Aren't you swell, Annabelle?"

The girls looked all around and then they looked up. Arnold swung himself down from the rafters.

Martha and Janie were indignant. "You aren't supposed to spy on people," Martha scolded.

"I was not spying. I was here before you were."

"Arnold," a voice called from the barnyard.

"Pa's in from the pasture!" Arnold exclaimed.

"Now why is he back so soon?" Martha asked. "Do you suppose he broke the mower?"

"Let's go see," Arnold suggested.

The three of them raced to the barn where Paul was working. Their father was showing him a metal tab.

"That's Rosebud's earclip!" Arnold exclaimed. "Where did you find it?"

"I found Rosebud. I mean I found her skeleton. I was mowing at the far end of the pasture and I noticed Trixie sniffing around by the fence. She found a pile of bones."

Arnold was unconvinced. "What happened to her?" he demanded.

"I think Rosebud got out of the barn that night of the hailstorm. She found her way out to the pasture so that she could be with the other cows. You know how we leave the gate open at night so the cows can come in by themselves in the morning."

"But none of the cows were hurt. Why Rosebud?" Arnold asked.

"When the hail and lightning started, the calf must have got scared and caught her head in the fence. Either the hail was too much for her or lightning hit her. We seldom go down to the far end of the pasture; so we just never found out about it."

"Well, I guess that solves the mystery of Rosebud," Paul said. "That earclip proves what happened."

"That's why Delcie and I saw those hawks there Sunday afternoon. They were curious about those bones," Martha said.

Arnold stood fingering the earclip. "So it wasn't Thaddeus Baronski after all. I'm glad you didn't go to accuse him as I wanted you to."

"Naturally I couldn't accuse anyone of stealing a calf when I didn't have any evidence! Stealing is a serious charge," Mr. Martin said. "Don't take it too hard, Arnold. You can try again this fall with a calf."

"I don't feel so bad about the calf as I do about the way I accused the Baronski boys. I'm sure glad they didn't hear me talk about how neighborly I felt about them. Plowing for them even though I thought they were thieves!"

Mr. Martin nodded. "Never pays to be hasty to judge other folks' character."

After her father had gone back to his mowing, Martha turned to Arnold. "But what about the hide-out? Somebody used it. We found a rope and a bread crust there. If it wasn't the Baronskis' hide-out, whose was it?"

Arnold's face grew red. "I knew it wasn't the Baronskis' hide-out. It was mine. When Pa sent me to the back forty to plow or something, I used that little place to rest in. I left my knot-tying rope there and you found it."

"Then it was you that Delcie and I saw go in there, wasn't it? I mean the day we threshed."

"I suppose it was. Now you don't have to tell Pa about it. I will tell him myself," Arnold promised.

"We won't be a blabber mouse," Janie promised.

"Blabber mouth," Martha corrected her from force of habit.

Paul's only comment was, "I wondered sometimes why it took you so long to plow an acre. Come on. Let's get back to the barn. You can help me clean out the calf shed."

Arnold picked up a pitchfork and followed Paul to the back of the barn. Janie tagged along with them.

Martha went off by herself to the swing. She pushed herself gently with her toe. As she swung, she thought.

How silly all that build-up about a dyed calf and the hide-out seemed now! The Baronski boys were not thieves, or at least they had not stolen Rosebud. She still didn't know why the sheriff spent so much time there. But by thinking that the brothers were guilty, Martha had excused herself for the way she had treated Stefana.

To be honest, Martha told herself, she hadn't wanted to like Stefana in the first place because she was Polish and different.

Her conscience brought her up sharply. "Now wait a minute; you said, 'To be honest!'"

"Well, all right. To be honest, I didn't try to like Stefana because she was smart in school, better than I was. I knew I was supposed to be nice to strangers, but I didn't want to be nice to Stefana."

"Stefana might be fun to know," her conscience suggested. "She hasn't lived her whole life five miles south of Cummings, Indiana, U.S.A. She might have some ideas that you have never thought of."

The big question now was how to right the wrong. Stefana was in Gary. If she liked it there so much better than on the farm, she might stay until school started. That was almost three weeks off, and three weeks is a long time.

"This is an emergency," Martha decided, and she went up to her room and fished out the last of the candy she had stored away.

CHAPTER 12

Wednesday, August 16
THE ICE-CREAM FEED

"JOHN GOOD stopped this afternoon," Mamma informed the family at the supper table Tuesday night.

"That right? What did he want?" Mr. Martin asked.

"He wants to give the ice-cream feed for the threshing ring tomorrow night. He wondered if he could bring the ice cream over here since his youngsters have the chicken pox. It's getting so late in the summer, and he wants to be sure to get it out of the way before school starts."

"I don't see why we couldn't have it here. What do you think?" Mr. Martin loved company.

"I told him to go ahead and plan on it. Everybody will be outside most of the time; so I won't need to do a big house cleaning. He will bring paper plates for the ice cream. It won't be any trouble, really."

That was how it happened that the Martins entertained the whole threshing ring with ice cream.

Mamma had said that it wouldn't be much trouble. But she spent most of the day cleaning, starting early Wednesday morning. The linoleum had to be scrubbed and waxed. The kitchen and living room windows had to be washed. Clean shelf paper had to be spread in the cupboards.

"My goodness, Mamma," Martha protested as she dusted

116

behind the piano, "nobody is going to notice that we are doing all this cleaning."

"Some of the women who are coming tonight have never been in my house.' I want it to look halfway decent," Mamma said. "Now go upstairs and see that things are at least picked up. They may want to leave their babies on a bed up there."

Papa was just as bad. He had Arnold mow the yard and Paul rake the barnyard. He himself got out the long-bladed scythe and cut the tall grass in the orchard. In the afternoon he and the boys trimmed trees and burned brush.

"They'll never notice those things," Mamma said.

"I planned to do this anyway. Might as well do it to-day," Papa replied.

Mamma fixed an early supper. The boys asked why there was no dessert, and Mamma reminded them that they would have all the ice cream they could eat later.

"But that's *later*. It's right now I'm hungry," Arnold protested. So she opened a can of peaches for those who wanted them.

The cars started arriving at about eight and kept coming for the next hour. All of the men in the ring brought their families; there were about forty people, including the children. Martha would have been happier about the whole evening if there had been girls her own age in the group, but there were none. Too bad the Birkys didn't belong to this ring. Martha stayed inside the house with the women. The men and older boys sat on the grass in the back yard.

The children Janie's age played hide-and-seek in the dark of the barnyard. Martha heard their shouts:

A bushel of wheat, a bushel of rye.

Who ain't ready, holler I.

And then when the seeker gave up, he invited all those who hadn't been found to show themselves by shouting, "Ally-ally else in free."

When he was sure that everyone had arrived, John Good unpacked the ice cream. Eight gallons looked like a lot. "But you know how these men like ice cream. Do you think we have enough?" he worried to Mrs. Martin.

"They can just quit when it's gone," she said.

Mrs. Martin looked over the array of cakes and sighed, "Don't they look delicious? And fattening."

John Good and Papa had set up a table in the back yard. The men were served first. Mr. Good piled their plates high until they told him to stop dipping. Some of them allowed themselves a pile of ice cream as big as the mound of mashed potatoes Mamma put on the table for six people. Each man chose the kind of cake he wanted, and Mamma laid a big piece on top of his ice cream.

"Eat it up, eat it up," Mr. Good urged.

"We'll be back for seconds," the men said.

The men had finished going through the line and the children were about to start when one more car drove into the yard.

Mr. Good peered into the darkness. "Now who would this be? I thought everybody was here." And then when he saw the trio coming up the walk, he boomed, "Well, well, look who's here. Glad you could make it."

Mr. and Mrs. Baronski and Stefana joined the party. Martha stood behind a tree while her mother greeted them. "Isn't that funny," she thought. "I forgot that the Baronskis belonged to our threshing ring. And here is Stefana, back from Gary."

While Mr. Good dished up ice cream for Mr. Baronski, Mamma took Mrs. Baronski and Stefana into the house and introduced them to the other women. She showed them to comfortable chairs and fixed them up with plates of ice cream. Martha followed along, but stayed in the kitchen.

Stefana looked nicer than she had at school. She still had her long blond braids. Martha decided that it was her dress that improved her appearance. It was a pretty white and blue cotton and not the black that she used to wear all of the time. Even so, the dress was too long and did not fit properly at the waist.

118

Martha did not know quite how to approach Stefana. She got her own plate of ice cream and cake and sat down beside her.

"What shall I say?" Martha thought. "What shall I talk about? Does she feel unfriendly to me because of the way I talked to her last time?"

There was a pause while both girls took bites of ice cream. The silence was becoming awkward. Then both of them said in one voice, "Will you be glad when school starts?"

They looked at each other in surprise and burst out laughing. Without saying a word, they hooked little fingers and silently each of them made a wish.

Then Martha said, "Needles."

And Stefana replied, "Pins."

"Shakespeare."

"Twins."

After this little ritual, both Martha and Stefana were over their tongue-tiedness. They chattered away about school and books and Miss Williams. Stefana said that she had been trying to learn to play ball. Her brothers had been trying to help her before they had returned to Gary. And she had an idea for a playhouse. Why couldn't they make one in the ditch along the side of the school ground? Then they could have an upstairs and a downstairs. Martha had never thought of such a perfectly perfect arrangement. They were sure they couldn't wait until school started to try the idea.

Stefana said, "I have just finished reading the best book, *Anne of Green Gables.*"

Martha squealed, "Oh, that's my favorite! How did you like the part where Anne hit Gilbert over the head with her slate because he called her 'Carrots'?"

Stefana exclaimed, "Oh, I just died at that part!" She helped herself to a bite of ice cream. "I have been reading a lot this summer."

An idea clicked in Martha's mind. "Say, where did you get your books?"

119

"Miss Williams lets me have the key to the schoolhouse so that I can use the library," replied Stefana.

"Were you in there about three weeks ago when I went to get a book?"

Stefana put down her spoonful of ice cream and opened her eyes wide. "Was that you!"

Martha nodded.

"I was scared to death," Stefana confessed. "I heard your key in the lock and hid because I didn't know who it would be. I didn't want to talk to anybody."

"And I was scared to death of you! To think how I tiptoed out of there and ran like a scared pup."

The girls choked on their ice cream, trying to keep from laughing. Mrs. Martin, who was visiting with the other women, gave Martha a scolding look.

"Come up to my room," Martha urged. "I have a letter from Miss Williams to show you."

After they had discussed the letter and admired Miss Williams completely, Martha got out a suitcase full of Mamma's old, old clothes and they played dress-up. There were shoes and dresses that had gone out of style. Martha gave Stefana her favorite things to wear, the long black dress with twenty-nine buttons down the back and the high top shoes.

When the party broke up and Stefana had to go home, Martha walked with her to the car.

Stefana whispered to Martha, "I'm sorry about the certificate. I didn't deserve it since I wasn't even in school for the full year."

Martha said, "That's all right. You deserved it." And for the first time she realized that this was true. Stefana had deserved the certificate. Martha added, "And next year I'll try to win it again."

Stefana's last words were, "You come to my house tomorrow and we will play dress-up with my things."

"I'll be there," Martha promised. "Cross my heart and hope to die."

As she went back to the house, Martha wondered what kind of clothes Stefana played with. Long black dresses? Fringed shawls? Martha hurried up to her room. She wanted to get to bed so that she could dream about the pleasant future that lay ahead for her and Stefana. Now she had a friend who lived close by.

Thursday morning seemed endless. Martha did her chores and practiced. She read a while. Then she sat down in the swing to wait for the afternoon to come.

Finally the mail came and Martha went for it. There was a package from Sears, Roebuck and Co.

"Paul's overalls came," she told her mother and laid the package on the window seat.

After dinner Paul asked, "Did my order come from Sears?"

"Oh, yes, I almost forgot about it," Martha said, and she got the package for him.

"Come and see my new overalls," Paul called to the family.

"What's so exciting about overalls?" Arnold griped, but everyone came for a look.

Paul opened the package. There were, in addition to the overalls, two small, narrow boxes. He held one out to Martha. "This is for you."

Martha was surprised. Janie was excited. This had been a secret that Paul had confided only to her.

"Open it, Marty. You'll just die! It's such a pretty w——," but Paul clapped his hand over her mouth.

The box opened under Martha's fumbling fingers. As the whole family looked on breathlessly, she lifted out a wrist watch.

Immediately she knew that the watch was for practicing the piano. This was something she had never even day-dreamed about, a real, ticking, running, time-telling watch. Not another girl at Indian Grove had a watch. Although this was the nicest present he could have given her, Martha could not find the right words to say "thank you."

"I'll practice very hard and always have a good lesson," she said. Paul seemed satisfied with that.

While the family was admiring the watch, Martha saw Paul slip the other box into his pocket. When he went outside, she stopped him on the back steps.

"What's in the other box?" she asked.

Paul laughed. "You may never know. But then again you may find out soon."

That was all he would say.

Martha hurried to the Baronskis' that afternoon. All the way down, she wondered what she should do about her new watch. Should she show it to Stefana and possibly make her feel unhappy because she did not have one? Or should she not show it and lose the pleasure of sharing a lovely possession? For the time being, Martha put the watch in her pocket.

Stefana had been watching for Martha and ran to meet her as soon as she saw her coming. Both had looked forward to the visit so much that both were tongue-tied again when they actually got together. What had they chattered about at such length last night? After they had said "hello" and "hot, isn't it?" there seemed nothing more to talk about. To break the ice Martha pulled out her new watch. Immediately, Stefana exclaimed over it, complimenting Martha on her beautiful gift. Martha had to tell her all the details of how she happened to own it. By that time they were in the Baronski kitchen and Stefana called Mrs. Baronski to admire the watch, also.

Then Stefana reminded Martha that they were to play dress-up. Stefana hurried her upstairs and into her bedroom. There spread out on the bed Martha found the beautiful Polish holiday costume. Stefana stood smiling as Martha tried to find words to say how pretty she thought it was.

Stefana insisted that she put it on. "See how you look in it. It was my great-grandmother's."

"No, it's yours. You wear it," Martha said with her fingers crossed, for she was dying to try on the dress.

Stefana insisted, and presently Martha stood before the

mirror dressed in the traditional Polish folk dress. The skirt was long and full, made of gold- and red-striped material. A white apron with red flowers was tied over this. The white blouse was cut full, with long flowing sleeves. Over the blouse Martha wore a bodice of red and black stripes. The bodice had a pretty pleated peplum around the bottom edge.

Then there was the headpiece! It looked like gold and silver metal lace, and the lace was dotted with shining stones of various colors.

Martha pirouetted before the mirror. "I feel like a queen. Oh, I love it!"

"If you were a married woman, you would wind your braids around your head and put the headdress over them," Stefana explained. "And you should have red or black stockings and black shoes."

Martha looked at her unqueenly bare feet.

"Now," Stefana continued, "watch me." She skipped away, keeping time to a tune that she hummed.

In ten minutes the girls, breathless but full of giggles were skipping down the length of the upstairs hall.

After they had put the dress away, they lay on their backs on Stefana's bed. They started talking about themselves: their favorite foods, their favorite relatives, the girls at school, and the boys. Stefana confessed that she hated her blond braids and wished she could wear her hair long and loose as Dorothy Johnson wore hers.

Martha stored this bit of information away to use on the first day of school. She planned to go to Dorothy and say, "Stefana loves your hair, but she is too shy to tell you herself," and Dorothy would beam, for she loved compliments. Maybe she would feel friendlier toward Stefana then.

"So you don't like braids," Martha said to Stefana. "Let me tell you what I don't like about myself. I hate and despise my greenish-brown eyes."

Stefana sat up and stared into Martha's eyes. "Why, Martha Martin! You have lovely hazel eyes."

"Hazel? Are my eyes hazel? You make them sound

pretty." Martha ran to look in the mirror. Her greenish-brown eyes, now made lovely by the adjective hazel, stared back at her. Martha made a mental note of this information, too. The next time that Arnold referred to her green cat eyes, she would say proudly, "Hazel eyes, if you please."

Later that afternoon they made plans for the school year. Stefana wanted more than anything else to be a good ball player. Martha told her to come after supper and they could all play together.

"Now that harvesting is over, our brothers will have more time," Martha said.

"But Casimir and Thaddeus aren't home, you know, only on Sundays."

They started discussing brothers, then, and there was so much to say about that subject. To hear Stefana talk about them, Casimir and Thaddeus were quite ordinary brothers. They teased her and bossed her; and they did nice things for her, too.

Martha wondered about that rumor about the Baronski boys. Had they been in trouble with the Gary police? She would have liked to have asked Stefana, but she felt she didn't know her quite well enough. Papa would probably tell her that she must never mention it.

When five o'clock came, Martha had to start home. The girls felt that they hadn't even begun to get acquainted. Stefana promised to visit Martha the next afternoon.

Martha walked home in a glow of happiness. Stefana was a girl to love, a sister who could share her every secret, a bosom friend right out of *Anne of Green Gables*. Her conscience reminded her that she had missed a summer of friendship by being so slow in getting acquainted with Stefana. Well, they would just have to make the most of the time that was left.

What should they do tomorrow? Tomorrow Martha would tell Stefana all about *The Romance of Paul Martin* and ask her if she had any suggestions for helping it along.

CHAPTER 13

Friday, August 18
MAMMA HAS VISITORS

"TOMATOES for breakfast!" Martha exclaimed in surprise.

Mamma nodded. "Louie Birky brought over a bushel this morning, and I still have apples to make into sauce to-day. The more you eat, the less I'll have to can."

Mr. Martin took a helping of sliced tomatoes and sugared them generously. "That's all right," he said. "I can eat them three times a day and for lunch."

Mamma looked at him enviously. "I can't understand it. You can eat sugar on your tomatoes, all the candy you can hold, pie and cake three times a day. And you are still thin as a broomstick. If I add an extra teaspoon of sugar to my coffee, I gain a pound. It isn't fair."

Papa said sympathetically, "That's the way my family is, the broomstick Martins. Your family runs more to a barrel shape. Look at your brother Will."

Plainly Mamma did not like the comparison. "But look at my sister Louise. She is slim as a willow."

"You mean she *was* slim as a willow," Papa corrected. "Did you notice that last picture she sent? Remember, you haven't see her for fifteen years."

Arnold spoke up. "But we'll go out next summer to see her for sure, won't we?"

Papa shook his head. "I don't see how we can, much as I'd like to. Even if the buckwheat turns out well and we make our mortgage payment this year, it will take us a few years to get back on our feet again."

Since Colorado was out of the question, the talk turned to a picnic at Lake Michigan. Every summer, at least once, and oftener if they had company from a distance, the Martins went to Lake Michigan. With less than a month of summer left, it was time to start planning the picnic.

"When shall we go?" Papa asked.

They discussed the subject the whole time during breakfast, but they could not come to an agreement as to when to have a picnic.

"Let's go tomorrow," Martha suggested because she knew they could not go today.

Mamma was aghast. "I couldn't possibly be ready by then. I have applesauce to make and tomatoes to can today. Let's go Sunday after church."

Paul shook his head. "The rest of you can go. Millers are having a family reunion Sunday and I promised Mary I would be there."

But the Martins would not consider a family picnic without Paul. Mr. Martin's question, "When shall we go?" was left unanswered.

After she had finished her piano practicing, Martha sat down to read in the swing. Just then she saw the mail lady drive away. A glance at her new watch told her that it was only eleven o'clock.

"The mail lady is early today," she thought as she went to get the mail.

There was a postal card for her mother. Martha would never have opened a letter not addressed to herself, but she reasoned that a postal card was meant for everyone to read. The news sent her flying into the house to find her mother.

"We are getting company! Uncle Will and Aunt Idy are coming. 'We should arrive about noon on Friday if our plans work out,' " Martha read.

Mrs. Martin was pressing hot applesauce through the colander. "Well, that's nice. It has been three years since they were here." Uncle Will and Aunt Idy lived on the other side of the state near Fort Wayne.

"There is a P.S. on the card," Martha reported, looking closely at the small writing in the margin. "Aunt Idy added a line around the edge. 'Had you heard that Aunt Sue died last month?' Who is—was—Aunt Sue?"

"Oh, you've heard me talk about her. Aunt Susan was my mother's oldest sister and is—was—the only one of her family still alive. My goodness, she must be—have been—in her nineties. I hardly knew her. She lived in Colorado near Aunt Louise."

"What will you fix for a good company dinner?" Martha asked, looking forward to a big meal.

"Arnold will have to go to town to get some things. We will have a roast and I'll bake an angel food cake since I have eggs ahead. Let's see, I'll bake bread. When did the card say they were coming?"

"Friday."

"Friday? Good. They will be here over the weekend. *Friday!* That's today." Mamma thrust the half-finished applesauce away. "What time is it? Go tell Arnold to catch a chicken while I put some water on to heat. My goodness, less than an hour to get a company dinner! Well, anyway they let me know they were coming, which is more than some of the relatives do."

The next hour was a flurry of potato peeling, chicken picking, dustcloth waving, and hair combing. Arnold worked on the chicken and Mamma on the rest of the meal. Martha set the house to rights, at least downstairs, and dusted. Janie flew upstairs and to the milkhouse and back upstairs on errands for everybody.

At the last minute the girls and Mamma put on fresh dresses and combed their hair. Mamma made Arnold change his shirt. When the relatives drove into the yard, the potatoes were ready to mash, the chicken was nicely browned, and the Martins were lined up at the house-yard gate to meet them.

Uncle Will stepped out of the car and caught Janie. "Hello, beautiful," he said as he lifted her high.

"Hello, george-ous," Janie replied, then shrieked as he held her suspended over his head.

"We were just talking about you at breakfast," Mamma said, and Martha noticed that she tactfully avoided saying that Papa had suggested that Uncle Will was shaped like a barrel. Martha, looking him over now, decided that Papa had been nearly right. On the other hand, Aunt Idy was on the broomstick side, tall and straight, finished off on top with a long, but pleasant face. How was it that broomsticks married barrels, Martha wondered.

Paul and Papa came in from plowing. They were surprised to find company and Papa was especially pleased.

"We are just ready for dinner," Mamma said. "Come wash up and I'll get it on the table. Isn't it lucky that the men are working at home instead of haying someplace else?"

Conversation at the dinner table was a catching up on news that had not been written on weekly postal cards that passed between the two families. They discussed relatives whom Martha had never heard of before. Uncle Will seemed especially fond of talking about his granddaughter, Frances.

"Do you take piano lessons, Martha?" he asked.

"Yes, Uncle Will."

"So does Frances. Her teacher says she is the best pupil she has. And Frances is only twelve years old."

Papa said, "I've an idee that Frances is a pretty fine granddaughter."

Janie asked, "Why does Papa always say, 'I've a nighty'? He's always talking about his nighty."

Everyone laughed at Janie, and Arnold confessed that he, too, used to think that Papa said that when what he meant was "I have an idea."

Martha wanted to shout, "I'm eleven and I'm important. Why doesn't anyone notice me?"

Instead she said, "Paul has a girl."

The effect was more than Martha had anticipated. Paul choked on his mashed potatoes and Arnold snickered. Mamma looked shocked and Papa came as near glaring at her as he had ever glared at anybody.

Only Uncle Will seemed at ease with the information. "That right? I hope she's a good cook. Nothing beats a good cook for a wife." Then he went on to tell about how his son had married a good cook.

Uncle Will and Aunt Idy planned to stay only for the weekend; so the Martins made plans with them after dinner.

"We can drive around and visit the cousins this afternoon," Mamma said. "Kate and Louie will probably want you for a meal."

"And tonight I will take you to town for an ice-cream soda," Uncle Will promised Mamma. "And before we go, remind me to give you something. I have a surprise for you."

"A surprise for Mamma?" Janie asked. Martha knew what Janie was thinking. All the surprises were usually for Janie and Martha.

Uncle Will laughed. "This surprise is for Mamma, but she might share it with you."

Uncle Will was Mamma's oldest brother, and she sometimes remarked that she could not quite get over feeling like a little sister, even though she was over forty years old.

"What shall we do tomorrow?" Paul asked, suddenly interested in the conversation.

"Tomorrow we will have a picnic at Lake Michigan," Papa said firmly, glad to have such a good excuse for going.

Aunt Idy and Mamma did the dinner dishes, and then Mr. and Mrs. Martin and their guests prepared to visit the relatives.

"We'll be home about five," Mamma said. "You might put some potatoes on about then and I'll make a quick meal when I get home."

After they had gone, Martha wondered what she could

do to make an impression on her uncle. She wished she were good at something so that she could compare with Frances. However, even if she would practice all afternoon, she would not be ready to compete in the field of piano playing.

"Maybe I could cook something!" she decided with what she considered great inspiration. "What could I make that would amaze everybody and make my family proud of me?"

At that moment she saw Stefana coming through the front gate. Martha had almost forgotten about her new friend with the excitement of having company. She ran to meet her and told her about her problem. Did Stefana have any suggestions for making something spectacular? Together they looked through the cookbook.

"How about a Lady Baltimore cake?" Stefana asked.

"Is it chocolate?"

"No, not in the picture."

"Then it won't do. If it's a cake, it has to be chocolate for our family. Why don't I try cream puffs? 'Lovely golden cream puffs with delicious filling,' it says here."

The two of them decided that cream puffs were exactly right. They would be different and impressive. Neither of them had ever made cream puffs and they couldn't remember that their mothers had ever made them.

Martha said, "This sounds like a very simple recipe. Just butter, eggs, flour, and salt. How can we miss?"

They stirred up the batter quickly, checking to make sure that they had all the ingredients this time. Martha told Stefana about her baking powderless cake.

The cream puffs were ready to put into the oven when Martha realized that she should have started the cookstove earlier so that the oven would be hot. Quickly she put cobs into the stove and got a good fire going.

"Preheat the oven to 400 degrees," the recipe said.

Martha slipped her pan of cream puffs into the oven when the thermometer read only 200 degrees. "They can get started while the oven heats up," she said.

Twenty minutes later, with Stefana peering over her shoulder, Martha opened the oven door to take a look at her cream puffs. A dozen flat pancakes lay spread wide on the pan.

Martha stared at them in dismay. "I guess it was important to have the oven hot *before* I put them in."

She called to Janie, "Take these cookies out to Arnold and Paul." To Stefana she explained, "I would like to have these eaten up before the folks come home. Here, have one."

Janie did as she was told and came back to report: "Arnold said to tell you that you make very sing-u-lar cookies. What's singular?"

Martha knew what a singular noun was, but she had never heard of a singular cooky. They looked up the word in the dictionary on the library table. "Singular: pertaining to a single unit or individual; hence, strange, odd, queer."

"I guess he means queer," concluded Stefana.

"They do taste funny," Janie admitted.

At five o'clock, Stefana went home. After Martha had told her good-by she thought, "Oh, dear. I didn't have time to tell her about *The Romance of Paul Martin.* I'll bet she would have had some good ideas for hurrying it along."

Martha peeled the potatoes and put them on to boil. At a quarter past five, her parents were still not home.

"I had better start something else," Martha decided. She cut ham for frying and opened a can of her mother's new sweet corn. She stirred up a batch of chocolate pudding and set the table. With the applesauce that Mamma had made that morning and the tomatoes that Mamma wanted eaten, Martha thought they would have enough to eat.

"I do wish those cream puffs had turned out well. This is such an ordinary meal," Martha told Janie.

The potatoes were done by that time, and Martha set them back so that they would not burn. She sent Janie out to stand by the mailbox to watch for their parents. In a few minutes Janie rushed in to report that she could see the car coming down by the bridge.

"Janie, will you start pumping? We will make lemonade. We want very cold water."

Martha cut the lemons into circles and mashed them into the sugar with the wooden potato masher. Then she helped Janie pump. Just as they finished, the boys came in from milking and Mamma hurried into the kitchen.

"Good for you, Martha," Mamma said, glancing at the supper preparations. "We just couldn't get away from Aunt Fanny's." Mamma tied an apron over her Sunday dress and helped make gravy and get supper on the table.

Martha was quite unprepared for Uncle Will's and Aunt Idy's amazement. "I can't believe that you got this supper by yourself, Martha," Uncle Will kept saying. "And you are only eleven years old! Frances wouldn't dream of going ahead with a meal if her folks got home late."

Martha's own family looked at her with respect. Arnold opened his mouth to say something, evidently thought better of it, and then said, "And you should try the cookies she bakes, too." Martha looked at him closely, but she could not tell if that was a twinkle in his eye or just the glitter from his glasses.

Mamma said apologetically, "Why, I guess we take Martha's cooking for granted. We just expect her to do this if we are late getting home. She is really a very responsible girl."

Martha enjoyed the praise; it was pleasant to have the relatives find that there was something she could do as well as Frances. However, the praise from her own family was even sweeter. But she could not get over the fact that it had come so unexpectedly. "I didn't even try to impress them. I just did what I knew I was supposed to do," she thought to herself. Maybe approval was like happiness: you couldn't catch it if you ran after it.

"I'll take another helping of that excellent chocolate pudding," Arnold said with great politeness.

"I'm so sorry that I have no singular cookies to go with it," Martha replied.

Martha felt at ease with the world for the rest of the evening. She floated about in a cloud of good nature, offering to do dishes, offering to read to Janie, even offering to run an errand for Arnold. All offers were politely refused by her surprised family; so Martha sat and listened to Papa and Uncle Will talk about crops.

Arnold buried his nose in a book and Paul drove off without telling anyone where he was going. As soon as Mamma finished dishes, she sent the girls to bed so that they would be up early to help get ready for the picnic the next day.

Breakfast the next morning took longer because Mamma took extra pains to have a good meal for the company. She added eggs and toast to the menu.

"One nice thing about company," Martha said to Trixie as she shook the breakfast tablecloth by the back door, "they usually help with the dishes."

Trixie lapped her milk without making any comment. Aunts who helped with dishes were of no concern to her.

Aunt Idy not only helped; she shooed the girls out of the kitchen. Mamma and she liked to talk about things that young girls did not understand. To make doubly sure that they did not understand, they sometimes talked German.

"*Was für Liebschaften hat Paul?*" Aunt Idy asked.

"*Oh, er hat eine Freundin,*" Mamma answered.*

Martha knew well enough not to ask what they were talking about, but she suspected that it had something to do with Paul and Mary.

This morning, however, there was more than gossiping to do in the kitchen. Papa had said that they must start no later than nine-thirty for Michigan City. Otherwise, they would arrive at the lake too late to find a good picnic spot. All that Mamma would promise was that she would get ready as fast as she could. But it took time to fry chicken, make a

*Translation:
  "Does Paul have a love affair? . . ."
  "Oh, he has a girl friend."

cake, fix lemonade, butter bread, and make potato salad.

"Martha, you make the icing for the cake. And don't use too much milk for the powdered sugar."

Martha could not remember a time when she had not used too much milk for the powdered sugar, and it happened again this morning. By the time she had added enough powdered sugar to thicken the milk, she had twice as much frosting as she needed. She put the extra on graham crackers.

"Now what, Mamma?"

"Clean the celery, then dice the eggs into the salad, get a jar of pickles from the fruit cupboard, and pour coffee into the thermos bottle. Idy, do you want to turn the chicken? Janie, run to the milkhouse for cream."

Finally everyone was ready to go. Papa had been dressed and waiting for the last half hour. But it was he who delayed the party while he ran back into the house. He had forgotten to change his heavy work shoes for his town shoes.

"Hurry, or we won't get a good picnic spot," Mamma called after him, laughing.

Since there were too many for one car, Arnold rode with Paul in the blue coupe. The rest of the family fit into the Martin car, with Janie sitting between Uncle Will's knees.

On the thirty-five-mile trip to Michigan City, they lost Paul and Arnold; or Martha thought they had, for they never did see them on the road. The Martins stopped in Michigan City for bananas and grapes for the picnic lunch. Then they drove through town and out to the lake. Just as they drove into a parking place, another car pulled in beside them. There were Paul and Arnold—and Mary Miller was sitting between them.

"She begged so hard to come along that we let her," Arnold explained.

Mamma was pleased, but not at all surprised. Martha remembered now that this was Mary's week of vacation. Paul had brought his girl to meet his relatives. She had been willing to come. Was that important, maybe? Perhaps *this* was the day for *The Romance of Paul Martin* to reveal the answers to those often asked questions. Martha watched for some sign from them, but they said nothing.

Martha and Janie were too excited to stand still; so right after the introductions, they all started off to find a picnic table. The picnic itself was a great success. They found a table set back from the lake under the trees. No other picnickers were nearby.

Mary had brought fudge to add to the menu.

"Can she cook anything else?" Uncle Will asked Paul.

"Well, she has served me some good food, but as far as I know, her mother may have cooked it," Paul answered.

Janie said loyally, "She makes good fudge. Almost as good as Arnold's."

They teased Mary, knowing that she was a wonderful cook and knowing that she enjoyed being teased. Martha kept waiting for Paul to say something about an engagement. When finally they started packing the leftover food back into the baskets, Martha decided that he would probably announce the big news at supper.

After dinner they strolled around the park to see the flowers, the Dutch Mill, and the foot bridge over the lily pond. Papa said that he thought the park got prettier every year. They went through the zoo to see if there were any new animals. As they did every year, they all climbed to the top of the lookout tower for a view of the lake. This was the southern tip of Lake Michigan and the waves came rolling in from the edge of the northern sky.

Finally, they all went down to the beach to sit on the blankets in the sand. Paul and Mary went walking off down the long pier that extended over the lake. Martha and Janie would have followed, but Mamma called them back. So they took off their shoes and waded along the shore.

When Paul and Mary returned from the pier a half hour later, Janie and Martha went to sit with them on their blanket.

Janie was the first to see it. "Oh, Mary, you have a watch," she said.

"Such a pretty watch," Martha said to Mary. "Is it new?"

Paul put his hand over his mouth to cover a big grin.

Then Martha caught on. "Mary and Paul are engaged," she shouted.

There followed a general crowding around to look at the lovely watch and to offer congratulations. Mamma and Aunt Idy kissed Mary, and Uncle Will shook Paul's hand. Everybody wore big smiles. Martha was overwhelmed by the news, for she realized how important an occasion this was. *The Romance of Paul Martin,* as far as she was concerned, had finally come to a happy ending.

"This watch was in that other box you got from Sears!" Martha suddenly remembered the box Paul had put in his pocket. "I am glad I got to find out what was in it."

"Isn't it lucky that Mary decided that she wanted the watch—and me with it? Otherwise, Sears would have had to refund my money," Paul said.

Mary laughed. "I just couldn't resist the watch, even though Paul came with it." Then to everyone's astonishment she kissed him on the cheek in front of the whole family.

For the next half hour the talk was of Mary and Paul and their plans for the future. About the middle of the afternoon they all started for home. Paul took Arnold home; then he and Mary drove off to have supper at her house. Paul was excused from chores on this his important day.

"Since you don't get engaged every day, I'll do your share of the milking tonight," Uncle Will offered generously.

At suppertime they all declared that they could not eat another bite, but Martha noticed that everybody took a good helping of the sandwiches and lemonade that Mamma set out. For dessert they had crescents of watermelon that had cooled all day in the milk tank. Next to pie, cake, and home-made bread, Martha liked watermelon.

As they were sitting around the table after supper, Janie asked for the fifteenth time that day, "When are you going to tell Mamma about her surprise?"

Uncle Will, instead of saying, "Before we leave," as he had fourteen times before, now said, "Thanks, Janie, for reminding me. Wouldn't that have been terrible if I had gone off without giving your mamma her surprise?"

He reached inside his back pocket and for an anxious moment felt around for something, slapping here and there as though he had lost it. Then he pulled out a long envelope which he handed to Mamma with a ceremonious bow.

"I am too old for surprises," Mamma protested, but her cheeks grew pink and her eyes sparkly. She opened the envelope and pulled out a blue slip of paper.

"A check! For one hundred and eleven dollars and twenty-three cents. Will Zook, where did this money come from?" Mamma passed the check to Papa who looked just as surprised as she did.

Uncle Will shrugged nonchalantly. "Oh, just a little wealth I am dividing up with you. I was executor of Aunt Sue's estate and this is your share. She didn't have any children of her own, you know; so her thirty-seven nieces and nephews get the money. What are you going to do with it?"

"I don't know. I can't think. I've never before had a hundred dollars to spend as I wanted to. I guess I will use it to pay off the mortgage."

Papa banged his fist on the table. The noise surprised everybody, for Papa was not a fist-banging man. "No, you will not use it to pay off the mortgage. The only way I will let you spend it is on a trip to Colorado to see Louise."

Mamma looked pleased. "Good! We'll just plan to go to Colorado for sure next summer."

They all started looking at road maps and making plans for next summer's trip. Uncle Will had been to Colorado once, and so Papa wanted to get the benefit of his advice.

This had been a wonderfully special day, with Paul and Mary's engagement climaxing the whole summer. As for tomorrow—Martha felt that she could not wait for tomorrow to come. She wanted to see the look on Stefana's face when she told her about Mary's new watch.

CHAPTER 14

Monday, September 4
THE LAST DAY

MARTHA lay awake, taking a few minutes to stretch before she got up for breakfast. School would start tomorrow—what joy! Today was for counting hours, for being patient, for being bored. Whose idea was it to have a holiday on a Monday when kids should be in school? Papa and Arnold did not consider it a holiday. They would plow and sow wheat today. Paul would work on his rented land. Papa said Labor Day was for laboring.

The Baronskis treated the day as a holiday. They had not forgotten city ways entirely; so they were going to visit their relatives in Gary. Martha was envious of those Gary relatives who would have the pleasure of Stefana's company.

Getting to know Stefana was only one of the many good things that had happened this summer. Another was Paul and Mary's engagement.

Martha's daydream took her back to the Sunday after Paul and Mary had become engaged. They had gone to the church in town that evening as usual. Then instead of Paul's sitting on the men's side of the church and Mary's sitting with the women, they went in together to sit on the back row of the men's side. When they did that, everyone knew that Paul Martin and Mary Miller were engaged. How the heads turned during the church service! Young people and children, and even the grownups, kept looking back at them to see how they were behaving. Paul and Mary sat calm and unconcerned, as though they had always sat together in church. Afterward, in the women's cloakroom, the girls crowded around to admire Mary's engagement watch.

Martha glanced at her own watch, now. It was time to get up if she wanted to eat with the family. Martha daydreamed about school as she dressed. Reading, geography, ball games, Miss Williams—good. Arithmetic, walking to school—bad.

Martha joined the family just as they were sitting down to eat.

"Your turn to ask the blessing, Martha," Papa reminded her as the family bowed their heads at the table.

Martha tried to bring her thoughts from the Indian Grove School to the Martin table. "I pledge allegiance to the flag of the United States and to the republic—" Martha felt an uneasy stir around the table. Then Janie giggled.

"Could you think of a table prayer?" Papa asked.

Martha was embarrassed. "I guess I was thinking about school," she explained and said her usual prayer.

About the middle of the morning Martha and Janie were swinging idly in the back yard, wondering what to do. A car drove slowly by the house. Martha read the printing on the door, "Sheriff, Pleasant County."

"What is the sheriff doing out here again!" Martha exclaimed.

The car turned into the barnyard. "What is the sheriff doing at our place!" Janie echoed.

The girls stood by the yard gate to watch the sheriff stop at the milkhouse. He talked for a moment to Mamma and then he and Mamma drove out to the field, evidently to find Papa. The girls waited impatiently while nothing happened.

Ten minutes later, they saw the sheriff bring Mamma back and then drive off down the road.

Martha and Janie ran out to the milkhouse to find their mother.

"What did the sheriff want?" they shouted.

While she scrubbed out the milk pails, Mamma told them all about the sheriff's visit.

"He asked what we knew about the Baronski boys. That rumor was true. They had been in trouble in Gary. When they first moved there from Poland, they got mixed up with some car thieves. The police didn't know whether they were innocent and just in with the wrong company by accident, or whether they were really criminals."

"I don't think Stefana's brothers are crooks," Martha said.

"I don't either," Mamma agreed. "Anyway, the sheriff came out here to check with the neighbors to see how the boys had been behaving themselves. Of course, Papa gave them a good recommendation."

"Too bad they have to work in Gary again," Martha said.

"The gang they were mixed up with is in jail now, and the boys have convinced the police that they were really caught in a trap, not knowing the country and the language when they first came here."

Martha was glad to know that Stefana's brothers were no longer in trouble with the law. The girls went back to the swing, wondering what they could do to pass the time until school started tomorrow.

"Is Martha around?" a voice called.

"Here I am."

"Would you and Janie like to come with me to town?" their father asked.

Of course they would. Martha quickly put on her new green and white gingham school dress that Mamma had made Saturday. Should she wear her new school shoes they had bought when they bought the books? Yes. Martha tied Janie's sash for her and they were ready.

Papa called to Mamma as they passed her on the way to

140

the car, "Have supper ready when we get back." This was his way of saying that they would be gone most of the day.

Mr. Martin told the girls his plans as they drove out of the yard. "I thought we might look around at some farms for rent to see if we could find something for Paul to start farming yet this fall. The first stop will be down the road at the Warner place. Then we will go on to town. What do you girls want for lunch?"

"Hot dogs!" the girls shouted in one voice.

There was a growl from the back seat. Papa put on the brakes and stopped the car.

"You, Trixie, are a touchy dog. If you don't want to be around when the girls eat those hot dogs, trot on home." Papa opened the back door and Trixie took off with her stumpy tail pointed down.

They drove past a field of buckwheat and Martha asked, "Do you think our buckwheat will make it, Papa?"

Mr. Martin said, "I feel very hopeful about that buckwheat. Of course, it won't make as much money for us as corn would have. But buckwheat's a good price this year. We should be able to pay enough on the mortgage to keep the farm. Don't you worry about it."

Janie asked, "Papa, are we poor?"

Mr. Martin looked puzzled. "Well, no. But we are not what you would call rich, either. What makes you ask a question like that?"

Janie said, "Well, if our buckwheat is good and we aren't poor, could I have an ice-cream cone with my hot dog?"

Papa said he thought they would be able to afford a nickel for an ice-cream cone apiece for Janie and Martha. "Come to think about it, I'd like one myself, chocolate, of course."

Martha smiled. This was a good day, this last day of the buckwheat summer. Then she was startled by a thought that she had never thought before: every one of the days of this summer had been good. On those days when she had felt dreary, Martha decided that instead of saying, "What a dreary day!" she should have said, "What a dreary person you are, Martha Martin!" And then she should have done something about it. A person doesn't have to be dreary.

"Here is the Warner place," Papa said. "Let's take a look."

Martha and Janie jumped out of the car, eager to explore what might be their brother's next home.

*　　*　　*

Dear Reader:

When I was a girl, I used to read books like this one; and I always asked questions when I finished the book: "Well, what happened to the people afterward? Did they live happily ever after?"

I want to answer some of the questions of "what happened" to the Martin family and their friends.

Although the buckwheat crop turned out well, the Martins never raised it again. Corn was a more profitable crop. Eventually Mr. and Mrs. Martin retired from the farm. They now live in Illinois where they take care of the grandparents.

Mary and Paul were married soon after the end of this story. They lived in the Martin home for a few weeks while they painted and papered at the Warner house. Then they moved into their first home. When the Martin parents moved to Illinois, Mary and Paul came to farm the home place. As the little Mennonite church is no longer in existence, they attend the town church where Mary belonged before they were married.

Arnold's honeybees produced some lovely, dark honey; but he did not get rich from it. However, he did get through college and realized his desire to become a teacher. He married a college classmate and now teaches English at a university in New Mexico.

Martha also became an English teacher. She married an Oklahoman. They have two daughters who will soon be the ages that Janie and Martha were in the *Buckwheat*

142

Summer. They live in Kansas. You might be interested to know that Martha never became a concert pianist. She does have enough music to know when her young piano player is hitting the wrong note.

This letter is beginning to sound monotonous, but Janie also became an English teacher, married, and has two daughters. They live in Ohio.

Now when the family wants to play the game of remembering around the supper table at the Martin farm, they must come from New Mexico, Kansas, Illinois, and Ohio. Someone is always sure to say, "Remember the summer we were hailed out?" And someone will answer, "That was the summer Paul and Mary became engaged."

Stefana and her family moved away a few years after the buckwheat summer. Although the girls wrote letters for a number of years, eventually they lost track of each other.

Now you know that "they lived happily ever after." Of course, that expression is never quite true for real people. One cannot live a life in which *every* day is a happy one. For example, there were days when Martha felt that her family did not really appreciate her, even though she honestly knew better. In time she overcame this problem and went on to solve more grown-up problems.

I must, in all truthfulnes, report that Martha never did overcome her habit of burning the potatoes. Her husband and daughters even today sometimes turn up their noses when she sets a dish of burned potatoes on the table.

But she says, "Well, a person can't just sit there and watch them boil, can she?"

THE END